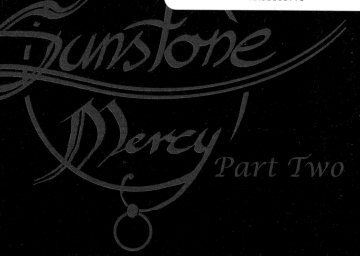

Sunstone
Mercy Part Two

Created by Stjepan Sejic

Published by Top Cow Productions, Inc.

Los Angeles

For Top Cow Productions, Inc.
For Top Cow Productions, Inc.
Marc Silvestri - CEO
Matt Hawkins - President & COO
Elena Salcedo - Vice President of Operations
Vincent Valentine - Lead Production Artist
Henry Barajas - Director of Operations

IMAGE COMICS, INC. • **Todd McFarlane**: President • **Jim Valentino**: Vice President • **Marc Silvestri**: Chief Executive Officer • **Erik Larsen**: Chief Financial Officer • **Robert Kirkman**: Chief Operating Officer • **Eric Stephenson**: Publisher / Chief Creative Officer • **Nicole Lapalme**: Controller • **Leanna Caunter**: Accounting Analyst • **Sue Korpela**: Accounting & HR Manager • **Marla Eizik**: Talent Liaison • **Jeff Boison**: Director of Sales & Publishing Planning • **Dirk Wood**: Director of International Sales & Licensing • **Alex Cox**: Director of Direct Market Sales • **Chloe Ramos**: Book Market & Library Sales Manager • **Emilio Bautista**: Digital Sales Coordinator • **Jon Schlaffman**: Specialty Sales Coordinator • **Kat Salazar**: Director of PR & Marketing • **Drew Fitzgerald**: Marketing Content Associate • **Heather Doornink**: Production Director • **Drew Gill**: Art Director • **Hilary DiLoreto**: Print Manager • **Tricia Ramos**: Traffic Manager • **Melissa Gifford**: Content Manager • **Erika Schnatz**: Senior Production Artist • **Ryan Brewer**: Production Artist • **Deanna Phelps**: Production Artist **IMAGE COMICS, INC.**

To find the comic shop
nearest you, call:
1-888-COMICBOOK
Want more info? Check out:
www.topcow.com
for news & exclusive Top Cow merchandise!

Sunstone, Volume 7.
ISBN: 978-1-5343-1886-1

Top Cow Productions Presents...

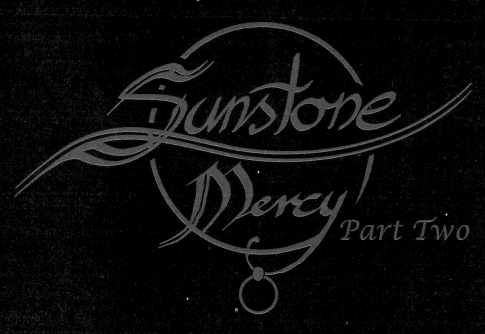

Sunstone Mercy
Part Two

Stjepan Sejic
Creator, Artist, and Writer

Stjepan Sejic
Cover Art and Logo Design

Matt Hawkins
Editor

Vincent Valentine
Editor

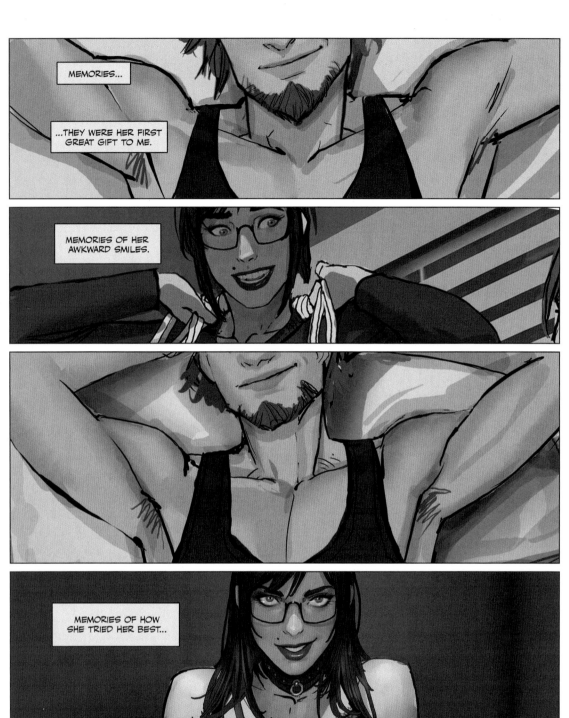

MEMORIES...

...THEY WERE HER FIRST GREAT GIFT TO ME.

MEMORIES OF HER AWKWARD SMILES.

MEMORIES OF HOW SHE TRIED HER BEST...

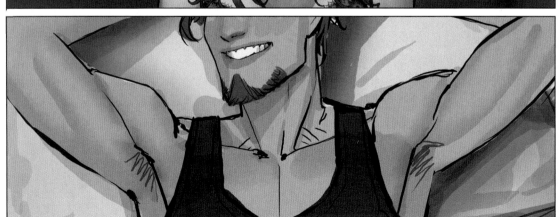

...MEMORIES OF HOW SHE MADE ME FEEL THAT DAY.
AND SURE, THESE MEMORIES WOULD FIND THEIR WAY INTO MY MASTURBATORY FANTASIES EVERY NOW AND THEN. I'M ONLY HUMAN, AFTER ALL. BUT...MOST OF THE TIME I WOULD JUST LIE IN BED THINKING OF IT ALL AND SMILING.
SMILING BECAUSE SHE WAS IN MY LIFE. SMILING BECAUSE SHE UNDERSTOOD ME. SMILING BECAUSE SHE TRUSTED ME ENOUGH TO PLACE HER SAFETY IN MY HANDS. THAT WAS WHAT MADE THOSE MEMORIES SO IMPORTANT. SO PRECIOUS.

IT WAS FEBRUARY 23RD. ON THE NIGHT BEFORE HER BIRTHDAY, I MADE A PROMISE TO MYSELF.
I WOULD GIVE HER SUCH MEMORIES AS WELL...
...I WOULD GIVE HER A REASON TO SMILE...
...THOUGH IN ALL FAIRNESS, I HAD A BIG HEAD START. TURNS OUT THAT DAY, SHE COULDN'T STOP SMILING IF SHE TRIED.

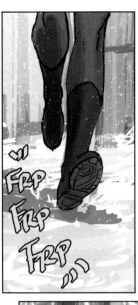
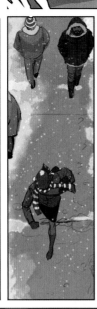
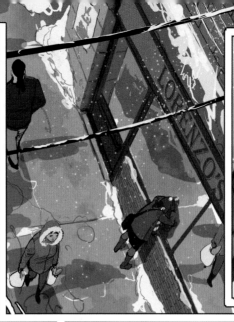

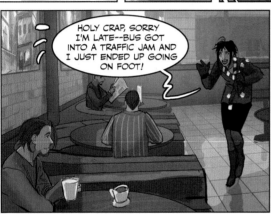

HOLY CRAP, SORRY I'M LATE--BUS GOT INTO A TRAFFIC JAM AND I JUST ENDED UP GOING ON FOOT!

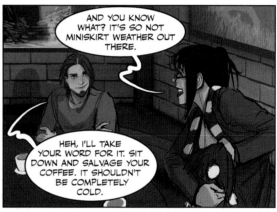

AND YOU KNOW WHAT? IT'S SO NOT MINISKIRT WEATHER OUT THERE.

HEH, I'LL TAKE YOUR WORD FOR IT. SIT DOWN AND SALVAGE YOUR COFFEE. IT SHOULDN'T BE COMPLETELY COLD.

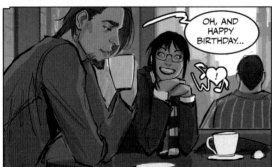

OH, AND HAPPY BIRTHDAY...

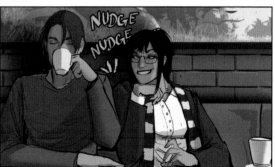

NUDGE NUDGE

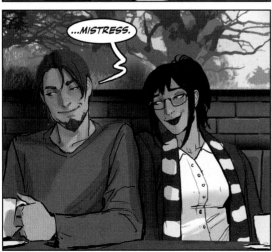

...MISTRESS.

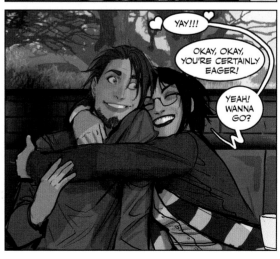

YAY!!!

OKAY, OKAY, YOU'RE CERTAINLY EAGER!

YEAH! WANNA GO?

WHAT'S THE RUSH? I THOUGHT WE'D FINISH OUR COFFEE, CHAT A BIT, WE GOT...
GLUG GLUG GLUG
...TIME.
SUBTLETY IS JUST NOT A WORD THAT EXISTS IN YOUR DICTIONARY, IS IT?
I DON'T REALLY HAVE TIME FOR SUBTLETY. SEE, THIS BIRTHDAY GIRL HAS BEEN THINKING ABOUT TODAY'S PLANS THE WHOLE WAY OVER HERE, AND IF SHE KEEPS SITTING LIKE THIS, SHE WILL LEAVE A PUDDLE ON HER FAVORITE SEAT.
AND YOU KNOW WHAT? THAT'S NOT MY PROBLEM.
OH, SO THAT'S THE WAY IT IS, HUH?
FINE!
WHAT ARE YOU DOING?
MAKING IT YOUR PROBLEM.
PLAY IT COOL!

IS... IS THAT A--
IT'S A GARTER BELT.
NOW, HOW DO I DESCRIBE THE EFFECT THIS HAD ON MY YOUNG FETISHIST SOUL?
YES!!!
OH, YOU'RE EVIL.
I KNOW.
ALSO... YOU WEREN'T KIDDING ABOUT LEAVING A PUDDLE. I THINK I FOUND YOUR LEAK, MA'AM!
MMMH...
...OH YEAH? WELL I THINK I FOUND A CORK.
SO WHAT I'M THINKING IS, WE GO TO YOUR PLACE AND PUT THAT CORK TO A GOOD USE AND DO SOMETHING ABOUT MY LEAK, OKAY?
R-RIGHT!
I'LL JUST PAY FOR THE COFFEE AND WE'LL...
...UH.
YEAH. AND I'M THE EAGER ONE.
RIGHT. SO MAYBE, LIKE, A FIVE-MINUTE TALK ABOUT YOUR COMPUTER LESSONS THEN?
HEH, SURE.
AND THEN WE'LL DO THE THING!

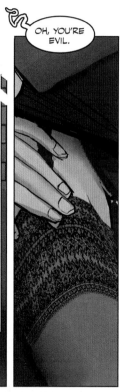

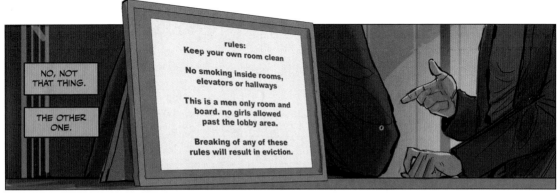

NO, NOT THAT THING.

THE OTHER ONE.

rules:
Keep your own room clean

No smoking inside rooms, elevators or hallways

This is a men only room and board. no girls allowed past the lobby area.

Breaking of any of these rules will result in eviction.

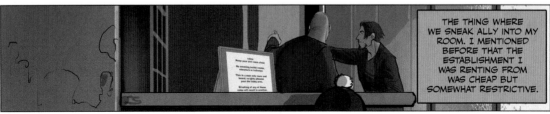

THE THING WHERE WE SNEAK ALLY INTO MY ROOM. I MENTIONED BEFORE THAT THE ESTABLISHMENT I WAS RENTING FROM WAS CHEAP BUT SOMEWHAT RESTRICTIVE.

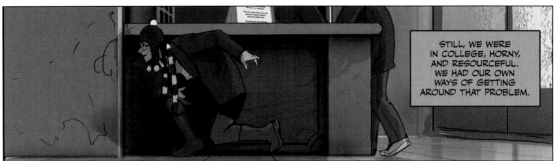

STILL, WE WERE IN COLLEGE, HORNY, AND RESOURCEFUL. WE HAD OUR OWN WAYS OF GETTING AROUND THAT PROBLEM.

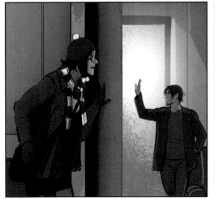

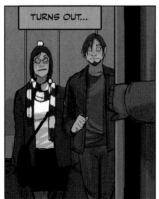

TURNS OUT...

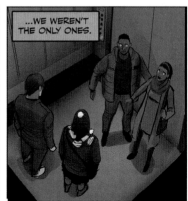

...WE WEREN'T THE ONLY ONES.

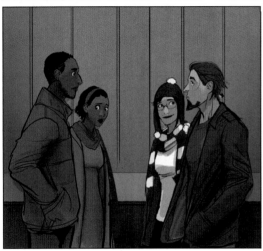

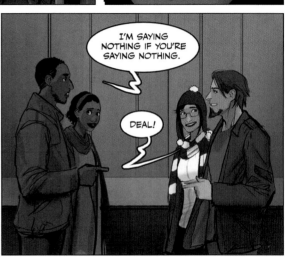

I'M SAYING NOTHING IF YOU'RE SAYING NOTHING.

DEAL!

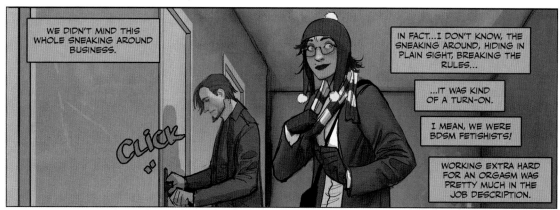

WE DIDN'T MIND THIS WHOLE SNEAKING AROUND BUSINESS.

IN FACT...I DON'T KNOW, THE SNEAKING AROUND, HIDING IN PLAIN SIGHT, BREAKING THE RULES...

...IT WAS KIND OF A TURN-ON.

I MEAN, WE WERE BDSM FETISHISTS!

WORKING EXTRA HARD FOR AN ORGASM WAS PRETTY MUCH IN THE JOB DESCRIPTION.

Click

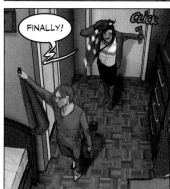

FINALLY!

Click

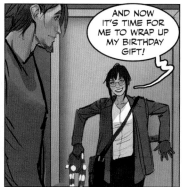

AND NOW IT'S TIME FOR ME TO WRAP UP MY BIRTHDAY GIFT!

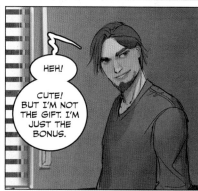

HEH!

CUTE! BUT I'M NOT THE GIFT. I'M JUST THE BONUS.

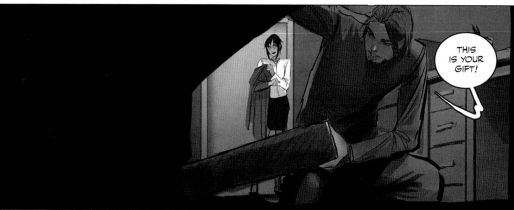

THIS IS YOUR GIFT!

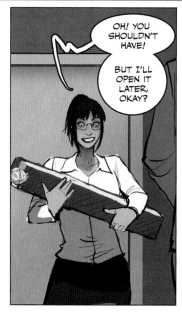

OH! YOU SHOULDN'T HAVE!

BUT I'LL OPEN IT LATER, OKAY?

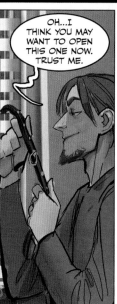

OH...I THINK YOU MAY WANT TO OPEN THIS ONE NOW. TRUST ME.

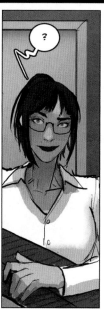

?

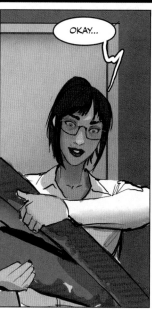

OKAY...

TURNS OUT IT'S EASY TO BUY A GREAT BIRTHDAY GIFT FOR A FETISHIST, ALL YOU NEED IS THE MONEY AND A LACK OF SHAME. SURE, IT MAY HAVE BEEN AN AWKWARD PURCHASE TO MAKE, BUT THE LOOK ON HER FACE...SO FUCKING WORTH IT!
...
FUNNY THING WAS, SEEING HER STANDING THERE ALL FLUSTERED, I COULD PRACTICALLY HEAR HER TRAIN OF THOUGHT. IT WAS CHUGGING ALONG AT FULL SPEED, LOADED WITH VISIONS OF CHAINS AND CORSETS AND BOOTS, OH MY.
ALL ABOARD!!
WHA...WH...BUT HOW? WHERE DID YOU GET THE MONEY?

I TOLD YOU I TOOK ON EXTRA WORK AT THE SHOP.
SO, WHAT DO YOU SAY, MISTRESS? TRY THEM ON?
I AM GOING TO FUCKING DESTROY YOU.
JUST, GIVE ME A FEW MINUTES, OKAY?
HEY, I'M NOT GOING ANYWHERE.
16:21
SO ARE YOU JUST STARING AT YOURSELF IN THE MIRROR NOW, OR?
HEY! IT'S A REALLY SMALL MIRROR! IT TAKES SOME EFFORT TO SEE THEM.
16:35
ALAN, I'M READY!
16:42

OH, THANK GOD. I WAS HALF A MINUTE AWAY FROM JUST LEAVING AND GIVING YOU AND THE BOOTS SOME MUCH-NEEDED PRIVACY!
UHUH... YOU WANNA RETHINK THAT, BUDDY?
I.... UH WOW...

...WHEN DID YOU GET THOSE?
WELL, I ALREADY HAD THE STOCKINGS. AS FOR THE REST, BIRTHDAY MONEY MEETS POST-VALENTINE'S DAY SALES. DO THE MATH!
HEH!
ANYHOW, NOW THAT I'M ALL DRESSED UP FOR IT, WHAT DO YOU SAY WE GET MY PARTY STARTED?
AND SO WE DID.
NOW, YOU'D THINK THAT OF THE TWO OF US, HER FIRST TRY WOULD BE NOTHING BUT SMOOTH SAILING...
...SHE HAD THAT MOOD ABOUT HER. A SORT OF DEVIOUSLY COLD LOOK THAT WOULD COME PAIRED WITH THIS SMIRK, AND YOU KNEW SHE HAD IT UNDER CONTROL...
...BUT I CAN TELL YOU FROM PERSONAL EXPERIENCE...
...CONTROL IS A SLIPPERY THING.
OH...
WHAT?
I... MAY HAVE PUT THIS ON WRONG.
KHM--
DON'T LAUGH! I'VE NEVER WORN THESE BEFORE!
FUCKING PORN PICTURES LIED TO ME!
PORN PICTURES?
YEAH... I MEAN, IT'S NOT LIKE I COULD ASK MY MOM HOW I'M SUPPOSED TO PUT ON MY FUCK ME GARTER BELT.
I SAW IT WORN LIKE THIS IN A BUNCH OF FETISH PHOTOS...
DAMN IT!

I PICKED UP ON THE SHIFT IN HER VOICE.
I KNEW WHAT IT WAS. AFTER ALL, I FELT IT MYSELF NOT SO LONG AGO.
H-HEY!
THE PRESSURE OF THE DOMINANT ROLE. IT REALLY GETS TO YOU IF IT DOESN'T GO AS WELL AS YOU HOPED.
THEN AGAIN, SHE WAS THE ONE WHO TAUGHT ME THAT AN OVERACTING SUBMISSIVE CAN HELP WITH THAT.
FINALLY, MISTRESS! I JUST CAN'T WAIT ANY LONGER!

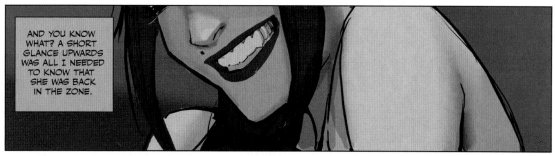

AND YOU KNOW WHAT? A SHORT GLANCE UPWARDS WAS ALL I NEEDED TO KNOW THAT SHE WAS BACK IN THE ZONE.

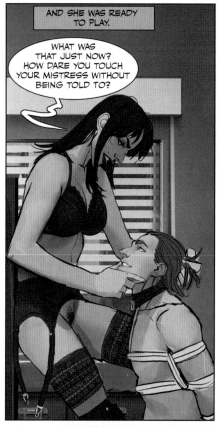

AND SHE WAS READY TO PLAY.

WHAT WAS THAT JUST NOW? HOW DARE YOU TOUCH YOUR MISTRESS WITHOUT BEING TOLD TO?

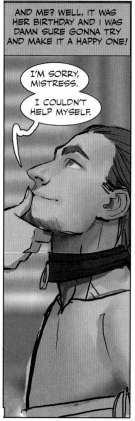

AND ME? WELL, IT WAS HER BIRTHDAY AND I WAS DAMN SURE GONNA TRY AND MAKE IT A HAPPY ONE!

I'M SORRY, MISTRESS.

I COULDN'T HELP MYSELF.

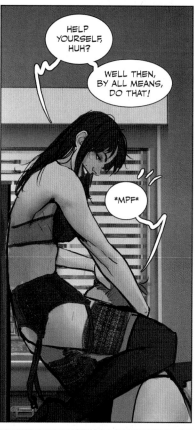

HELP YOURSELF, HUH?

WELL THEN, BY ALL MEANS, DO THAT!

MPF

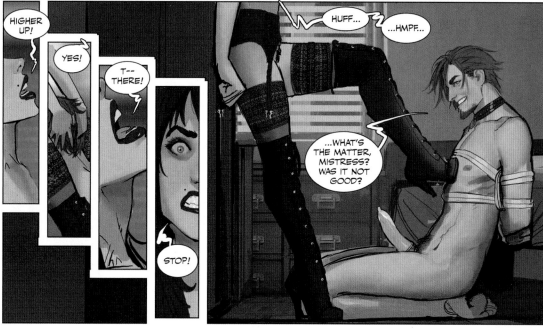

HIGHER UP!

YES!

T-- THERE!

STOP!

HUFF...

...HMPF...

...WHAT'S THE MATTER, MISTRESS? WAS IT NOT GOOD?

DON'T GET COCKY, PET!
IT MAY HAVE BEEN NO MORE THAN GLORIFIED PRACTICE...
BUT EVEN THEN, I SAW IT IN HER EYES.
HER DOMSPACE.
LATER IN MY LIFE, I HEARD SOMEONE SAY: A GOOD PERSON CAN MAKE ANY HOUSE INTO A HOME, BUT A GOOD DOMME CAN MAKE ANY PLACE INTO A DUNGEON.
WHEN I HEARD THAT, I THOUGHT OF MY DINGY ROOM. I THOUGHT OF ALLY'S BIRTHDAY, AND YOU KNOW WHAT?
I SMILED. I SMILED BECAUSE IT WAS TRUE.

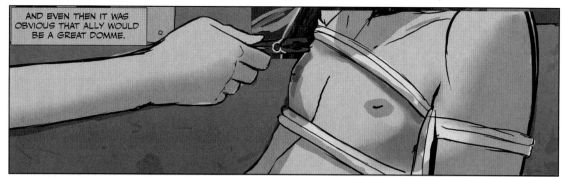

AND EVEN THEN IT WAS OBVIOUS THAT ALLY WOULD BE A GREAT DOMME.

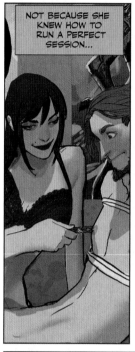

NOT BECAUSE SHE KNEW HOW TO RUN A PERFECT SESSION...

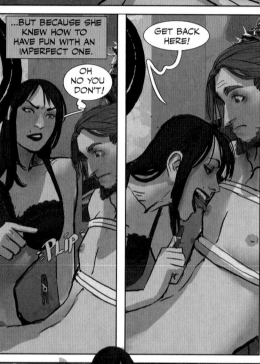

...BUT BECAUSE SHE KNEW HOW TO HAVE FUN WITH AN IMPERFECT ONE.

OH NO YOU DON'T!

GET BACK HERE!

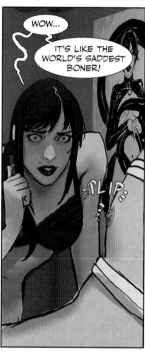

WOW...

IT'S LIKE THE WORLD'S SADDEST BONER!

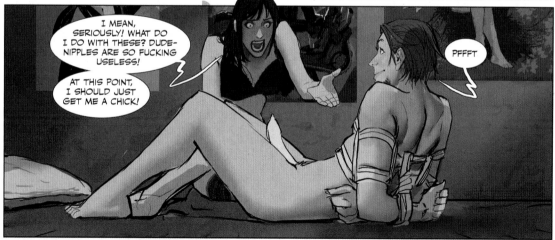

I MEAN, SERIOUSLY! WHAT DO I DO WITH THESE? DUDE-NIPPLES ARE SO FUCKING USELESS!

AT THIS POINT, I SHOULD JUST GET ME A CHICK!

PFFFT

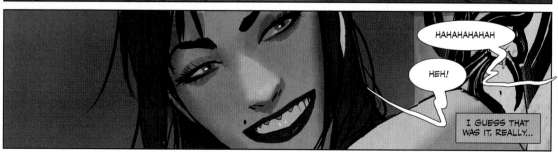

HAHAHAHAHAH

HEH!

I GUESS THAT WAS IT, REALLY...

...ALLY'S FIRST SESSION IN A NUTSHELL.
JUST LIKE MY FIRST TRY, IT WAS MESSY...
...FLAWED...
NOT YET!
...AND, YEAH... IT WAS AMAZING.
NOT...
AH!
N- NOT YET!
HEH!
AND JUST LIKE MY FIRST TRY, THE HARDEST PART OF IT ALL WAS HOLDING OUT UNTIL SHE GAVE ME HER PERMISSION TO COME.
A-AH AH, N-NO-- NOW!
BUT IN THE END, WE DID JUST THAT. ENTANGLED IN A STRAINED SPASM. WE ENDED THE NIGHT ON A SOMEWHAT MUFFLED HIGH NOTE.
MMMMPH!!!!
MMMNGHHH!!!

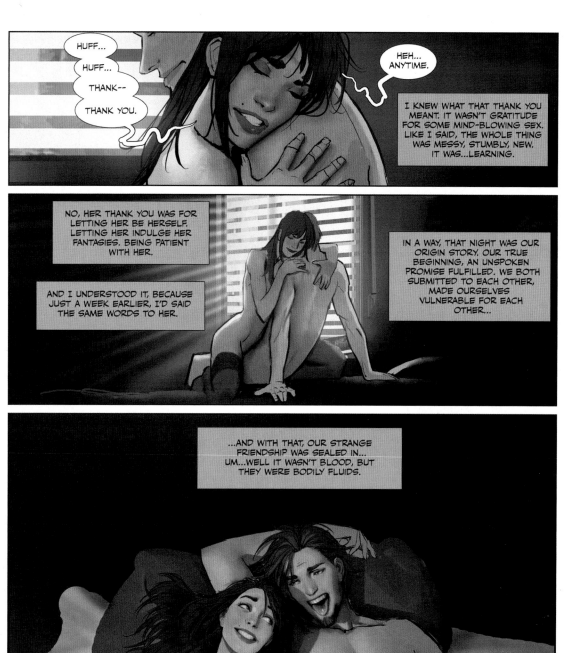

HUFF...

HUFF...

THANK--

THANK YOU.

HEH... ANYTIME.

I KNEW WHAT THAT THANK YOU MEANT. IT WASN'T GRATITUDE FOR SOME MIND-BLOWING SEX. LIKE I SAID, THE WHOLE THING WAS MESSY, STUMBLY, NEW. IT WAS...LEARNING.

NO, HER THANK YOU WAS FOR LETTING HER BE HERSELF. LETTING HER INDULGE HER FANTASIES. BEING PATIENT WITH HER.

AND I UNDERSTOOD IT, BECAUSE JUST A WEEK EARLIER, I'D SAID THE SAME WORDS TO HER.

IN A WAY, THAT NIGHT WAS OUR ORIGIN STORY. OUR TRUE BEGINNING, AN UNSPOKEN PROMISE FULFILLED. WE BOTH SUBMITTED TO EACH OTHER, MADE OURSELVES VULNERABLE FOR EACH OTHER...

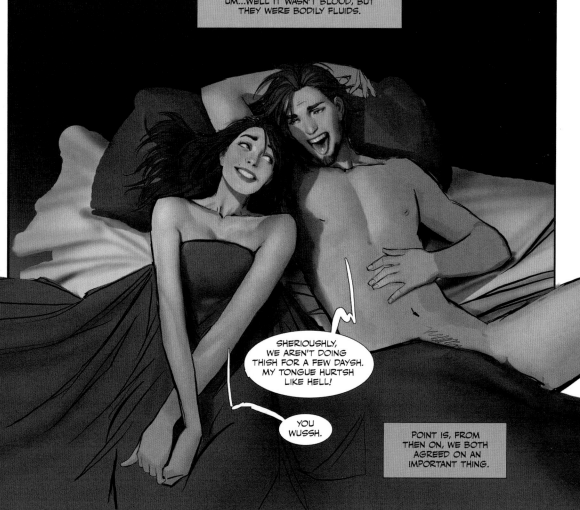

...AND WITH THAT, OUR STRANGE FRIENDSHIP WAS SEALED IN... UM...WELL IT WASN'T BLOOD, BUT THEY WERE BODILY FLUIDS.

SHERIOUSLY, WE AREN'T DOING THISH FOR A FEW DAYSH. MY TONGUE HURTSH LIKE HELL!

YOU WUSSH.

POINT IS, FROM THEN ON, WE BOTH AGREED ON AN IMPORTANT THING.

HAVING SOMEONE SPECIAL TO YOU IN YOUR LIFE IN ONE WAY OR ANOTHER CAN CHANGE YOU IN WONDERFUL WAYS...
MAKE YOU SEE LIFE IN A NEW WAY.

TURN THAT FROWN UPSIDE DOWN.
...I REMEMBER THE TIME WHEN WE HOWLED AT THE NIGHT!!!

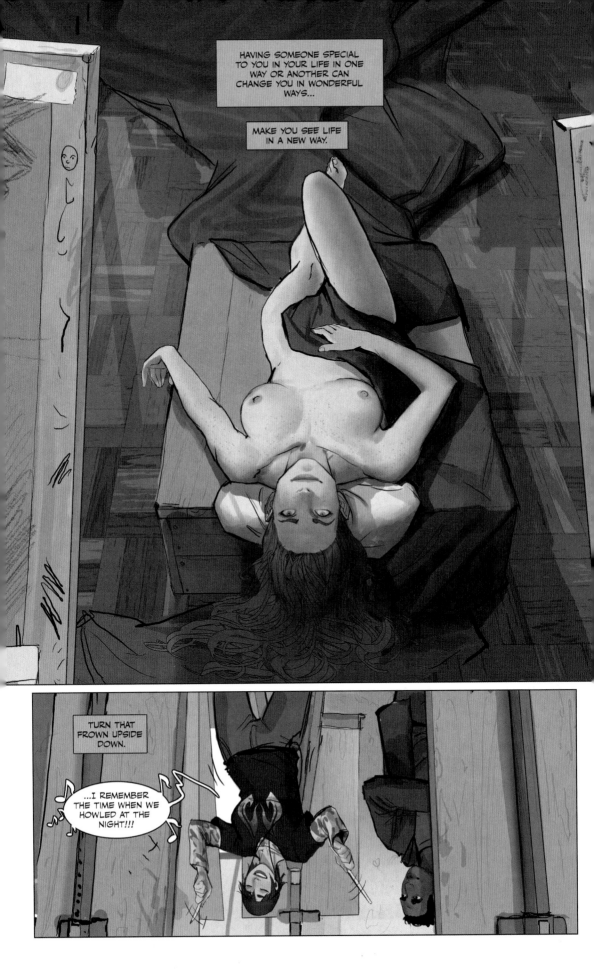

OKAY, WRAP IT UP, EVERYONE. TEN MINUTES.
MARIANNE, ONLY HEAVEN KNOWS WHY I WALK IN THE SHADOW OF MURDER OF CROWS--
OH THANK GOD!
EVERYONE MEANS YOU TOO, MISS MURPHY!
WAH! OH, WE'RE DONE?
YES.
YOU SURE ARE IN A CHEERY MOOD.
REALLY?
HM...
YEAH, I GUESS I AM.
HEH. IT'S SO WEIRD TO SEE A HAPPY GOTH.
HEY, I'M NOT A GOTH ANYMORE, I'M A METALHEAD!
SO THAT'S LIKE SWITCHING TO A LESS STRICT FORM OF RELIGION?

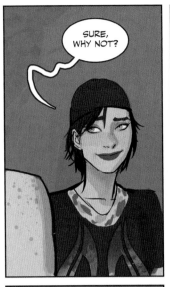

SURE, WHY NOT?

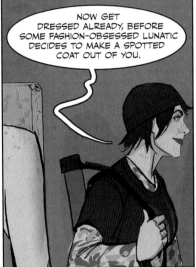

NOW GET DRESSED ALREADY, BEFORE SOME FASHION-OBSESSED LUNATIC DECIDES TO MAKE A SPOTTED COAT OUT OF YOU.

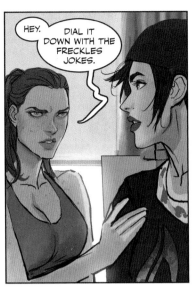

HEY.

DIAL IT DOWN WITH THE FRECKLES JOKES.

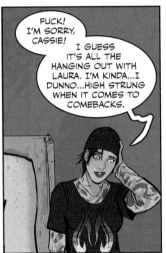

FUCK! I'M SORRY, CASSIE!

I GUESS IT'S ALL THE HANGING OUT WITH LAURA. I'M KINDA...I DUNNO...HIGH STRUNG WHEN IT COMES TO COMEBACKS.

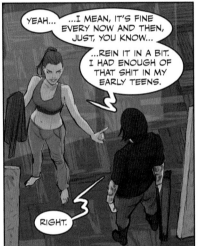

YEAH...

...I MEAN, IT'S FINE EVERY NOW AND THEN, JUST, YOU KNOW...

...REIN IT IN A BIT. I HAD ENOUGH OF THAT SHIT IN MY EARLY TEENS.

RIGHT.

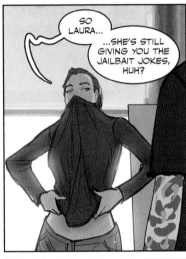

SO LAURA...

...SHE'S STILL GIVING YOU THE JAILBAIT JOKES, HUH?

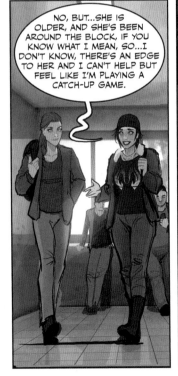

NO, BUT...SHE IS OLDER, AND SHE'S BEEN AROUND THE BLOCK, IF YOU KNOW WHAT I MEAN, SO...I DON'T KNOW, THERE'S AN EDGE TO HER AND I CAN'T HELP BUT FEEL LIKE I'M PLAYING A CATCH-UP GAME.

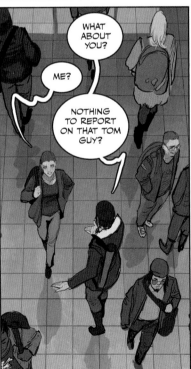

WHAT ABOUT YOU?

ME?

NOTHING TO REPORT ON THAT TOM GUY?

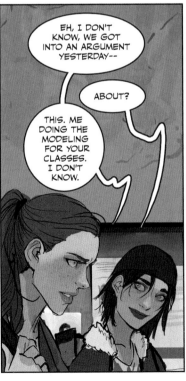

EH, I DON'T KNOW, WE GOT INTO AN ARGUMENT YESTERDAY--

ABOUT?

THIS. ME DOING THE MODELING FOR YOUR CLASSES. I DON'T KNOW.

SO WHAT DID YOU TELL HIM?
WELL, YOU KNOW, IF HE IS SO INSECURE THAT THE IDEA OF ANYONE ELSE SEEING ME NAKED IN A COMPLETELY NON-SEXUAL ENVIRONMENT SCARES HIM, THAT'S HIS PROBLEM.
AND WHAT DID HE SAY?
I DUNNO, HE WENT AWAY MUMBLING SOMETHING.
WHY DID YOU EVEN HAVE TO GO THERE? NOW MY MOOD IS ALL RUINED.
WOW, YOU REALLY LIKE HIM, DON'T YOU?
OH, FUCK OFF!
CASSIE AND TOM, SITTIN' IN A TREE--
I'M WARNING YOU.
MR. TOM WILSON, AND MRS. CASSIE WILSON--
STOP THAT!
HEH!

PFFT
HAHA HAHAH
SHIT, I HOPE THE BIG DUMBASS GETS OVER IT.
WHAT ABOUT YOU THOUGH?
HUH?
I MEAN, ALL THE TEASING ASIDE...
YOU HAPPY WITH LAURA?
HELL YEAH!

I MEAN, I'M SPENDING MOST OF MY TIME WITH HER JUST HANGING OUT. GETTING TO KNOW HER...
...WATCHING MOVIES...
...TURNS OUT SHE'S NOT A FAN OF OLD HORROR...
...TRYING OUT EACH OTHER'S FAVORITE FOODS.
ALSO, TURNS OUT I'M NOT BIG ON SUSHI.
BUT HEY, WE GOT OUR MUSIC.
HOLY SHIT! GOOSEBUMPS ON THE FIRST LISTEN!
TOLD YOU!
AND, OF COURSE, THERE IS THE PART OF GETTING TO KNOW EACH OTHER...
...THE COOL, UNEXPECTED STUFF.
YOU CAN HANG YOUR JACKET IN THERE.
RIGHT... UH...
...HEY, THE BIKER JACKET HERE?
WHAT ABOUT IT?
IT'S YOURS?
YEAH. LIKE IT?

I LOVE IT. I WAS ALWAYS A SUCKER FOR THESE. WANTED TO GET ONE FOR A WHILE NOW.
TRY IT ON!
!
OH YEAH! THAT'S THE STUFF!
JUST IMAGINE ME TAMING THAT WILD OPEN ROAD! WIND IN MY HAIR, A HYPOTHETICAL BIKE BETWEEN MY LEGS, HEH!
I MEAN, THE WIND IN YOUR HAIR MIGHT BE A BAD IDEA ON ACCOUNT OF IT BEING FEBRUARY, BUT THE BIKE DOESN'T HAVE TO BE HYPOTHETICAL.
I'M SORRY...
WHAT?!
BEHOLD!
MY SEEMINGLY ENDLESS FINANCIAL BURDEN!

HOLY CRAP!
YOU'VE GOT A HARLEY!?
I'VE GOT A HARLEY!
FIRST OF ALL, WHY DIDN'T YOU PICK ME UP FOR OUR DATE ON THIS!? AND SECOND OF ALL, HOW MUCH DO YOU EARN!?
WELL, TO ANSWER YOUR FIRST QUESTION: AGAIN, IT'S FUCKING FEBRUARY!! I GOT SICK AS A DOG JUST GOING ON THAT DATE IN A TAXI.
WUSS!
AS FOR THE SECOND QUESTION. I MAKE *PAY THE BILLS* MONEY. NOT *BUY A HARLEY* MONEY.
I COULD BARELY AFFORD THE REPAIRS ON IT!
BUT THEN...
HOW?
IT WAS MY UNCLE'S. MY MOM SAYS HE'S A BAD INFLUENCE ON ME, BUT THEN AGAIN, MOM IS CRITICAL OF MANY OTHER ASPECTS OF MY LIFE AS WELL, SO...WHO GIVES A SHIT, RIGHT?
UH, ANYWAYS. POINT IS, HE GOT IT FOR HIMSELF. SAID HE WAS GETTING READY FOR THAT MID-LIFE CRISIS DOWN THE ROAD. INSTEAD OF A CRISIS, HE GOT A KID AND BECAME ALL RESPONSIBLE AND SHIT.
HEHEHE.
A RESPONSIBLE PARENT!? OH MY GOD, THAT'S THE WORST!
SO, YOU LIKE IT?

LIKE IT? I FUCKING *LOVE* IT!
YEAH, S'OKAY!
OH FUCK YOU! IT'S AMAZING.
I MEAN, IMAGINE YOURSELF IN THIS JACKET...
...YOU RIDE THIS BEAST UP TO MY APARTMENT.
GO ON!

YOU HONK THE HORN?
IT'S BUSTED.
BELL?
NOPE!
YOU YELL! "HEY BABY! GET ON BOARD!"
AND THEN I GUESS YOU DO JUST THAT?
UHUH.
YOU SIT BEHIND ME LIKE THIS?
I...I MEAN, YEAH.
YOU GRAB ON TIGHT.
WELL, I WOULDN'T WANT TO FALL OFF.
MHM...
AND THEN...

WE DO SOMETHING DANGEROUS...

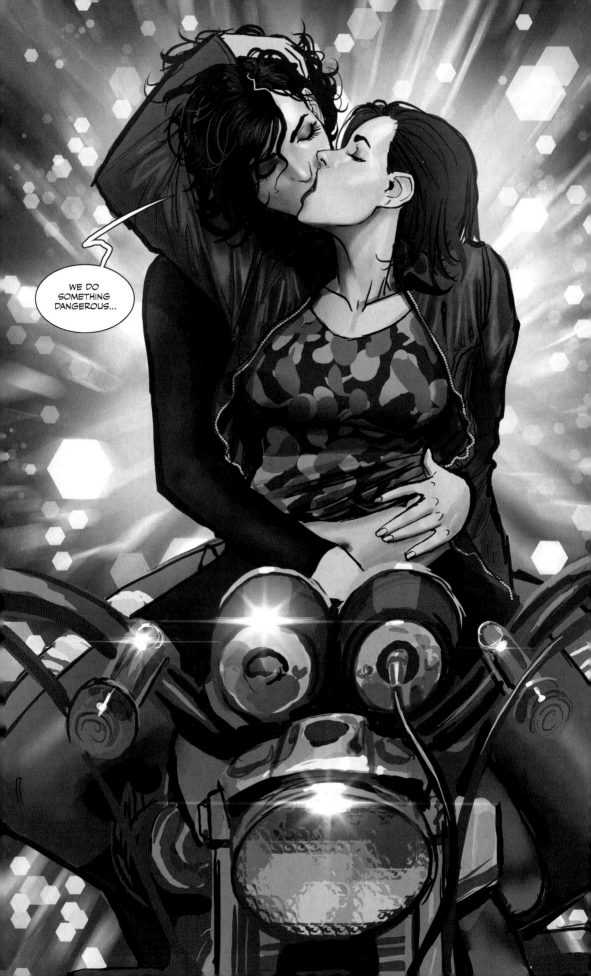

...AND...WELL IT WAS NICE.
KEYS
NICE...
...YOU HAD SEX!
NO...
...OKAY FINE, WE MADE LOVE. IT'S ACTUALLY BEEN A FEW TIMES NOW, SO YOU DON'T HAVE TO MAKE SUCH A PRODUCTION OUT OF IT.

SIGH.
OH MY GOD, WHAT?
NOTHING... IT'S JUST, I DON'T KNOW, I KINDA EXPECTED YOU'D TELL ME.
HUH?
I MEAN...I THOUGHT WE SHARED... YOU KNOW WHAT? NEVERMIND.
OKAY, FINE! WHAT DO YOU WANNA KNOW?
I DON'T KNOW, DID YOU DO, LIKE...LESBIAN STUFF?
CASSIE? WHAT THE FUCK IS "LESBIAN STUFF"?
YOU TELL ME! I'M NOT ONE!
OH FOR CRYING OUT LOUD, FINE!
COME ON! I NEED COFFEE!
I ACTUALLY NEED TO MEET TOM.
INVITE HIM!
OKAY, I'LL TELL YOU MY "LESBIAN STUFF" IF YOU TELL ME IF YOU AND TOM DID THE "STRAIGHT STUFF"!
GROW UP!
OH COME ON, HE'S NOT HERE YET AND IT'S A FAIR EXCHANGE!
WELL?
DID YOU LET HIM PLAY *CONNECT THE DOTS* ALL OVER YOU?
OH, BLOW ME!
OOOH! WAIT! I GOT A GOOD ONE!

DID HE SAMPLE YOUR GINGER ALE?
PFFFTT
YOU UNBELIEVABLE BITCH. HAHAHHAHAH!
FINE! YES, OKAY, WE DID IT.
NOW YOU!
ME WHAT?
WELL FOR ONE, TELL ME WHY YOU KEPT QUIET ABOUT IT.
AH.
I MEAN, YOU DIDN'T SHARE ABOUT YOU AND TOM, EITHER.
I... HUH...
YOU'RE RIGHT.
YEAH, NO! FUCK THIS, WE'RE NOT LOSING TRACK OF EACH OTHER JUST 'CAUSE WE'RE IN RELATIONSHIPS!
OKAY! GO ON, THEN!
YES, WE'VE DONE IT FOUR TIMES SO FAR. AND YES, HE DID, AS YOU PUT IT, SAMPLE MY GINGER ALE. AND BY THAT I HOPE YOU MEAN GOING DOWN ON ME!
OTHERWISE, YOU ARE INTO SOME WEIRD SHIT AND I WILL TEASE YOU ABOUT IT!
NOW YOU!

I DON'T KNOW, UM, THE FIRST FEW TIMES WE DID IT...IT WAS HAND STUFF, KISSING...UH, YOU KNOW...ORAL.
THE LAST TIME, HOWEVER, THE TIME WITH THE BIKE, LAURA WANTED TO TRY SOMETHING... UH...DIFFERENT.
I GUESS YOU MIGHT CALL IT, THE "LESBIAN STUFF!"
OKAY, YOU UM, PUT YOUR RIGHT FOOT UNDER ME.
RIGHT... AND RIGHT ARM YELLOW
HAHAHAH, HEY! STOP IT, THIS IS SERIOUS! I ALWAYS WANTED TO TRY THIS, OKAY!
LAURA...
THIS IS SO IMPRACTICAL!
OH MY GOD!
JUST SHUT UP AND MOVE IN CLOSER!

AND BELIEVE YOU ME, IT WAS IMPRACTICAL, LIKE, DON'T GET ME WRONG, BUT THE MOMENT OUR...YOU KNOW, NAUGHTY BITS TOUCHED, I'M NOT GONNA LIE, IT WAS ELECTRIC.
NOT...
NOT GONNA LIE, THIS IS THE STRANGEST KISS I'VE EVER GIVEN!
Y-YEAH! SAME!
AND AT FIRST, WE'RE NAILING IT, RIGHT? WE'RE HITTING THE SPOT AND IT IS AMAZING.

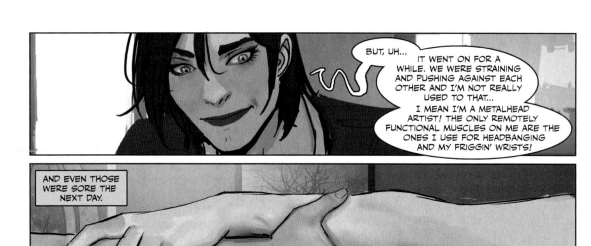

BUT, UH... IT WENT ON FOR A WHILE. WE WERE STRAINING AND PUSHING AGAINST EACH OTHER AND I'M NOT REALLY USED TO THAT...

I MEAN I'M A METALHEAD ARTIST! THE ONLY REMOTELY FUNCTIONAL MUSCLES ON ME ARE THE ONES I USE FOR HEADBANGING AND MY FRIGGIN' WRISTS!

AND EVEN THOSE WERE SORE THE NEXT DAY.

AND ALSO IT'S LIKE... WELL, YOU'RE TRYING TO KEEP THE CLIT STIMULATED, BUT IT'S A SMALL POINT AND WE'RE BOTH MOVING LIKE CRAZY... SO IT'S KINDA LIKE TRYING TO DO PRECISION WORK WHILE RIDING ON A ROLLERCOASTER...

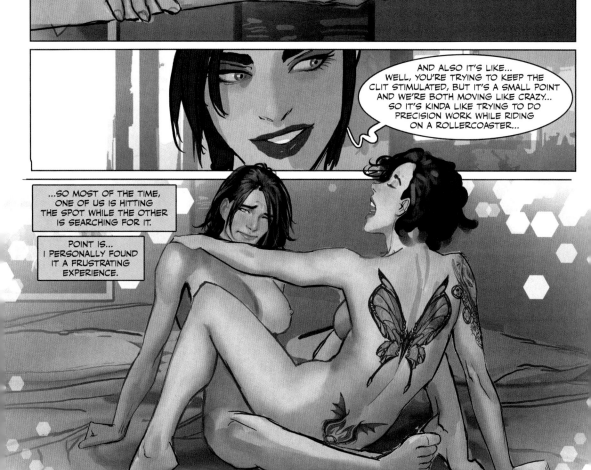

...SO MOST OF THE TIME, ONE OF US IS HITTING THE SPOT WHILE THE OTHER IS SEARCHING FOR IT.

POINT IS... I PERSONALLY FOUND IT A FRUSTRATING EXPERIENCE.

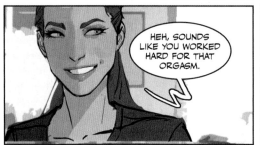

HEH, SOUNDS LIKE YOU WORKED HARD FOR THAT ORGASM.

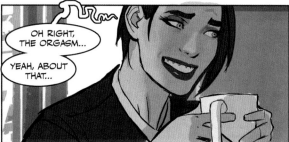

OH RIGHT, THE ORGASM...

YEAH, ABOUT THAT...

REMEMBER HOW I SAID I WASN'T USED TO THE STRAINING AND THE PUSHING?
YEAH, I MEANT THAT!
MTHRFCK!!!!
MARIANNE?!
MMMMMNNGH!!! CRAMP!!!
CAN-- UH, CAN I HELP?
NO JUST...NGH!!! LET ME FETAL POSITION MY WAY THROUGH THIS!
OH FUCK IT HURTS!!!

THAT WON'T HELP.
LET ME MASSAGE IT!
NO, NGH! JUST LET ME DIE OF EMBARRASSMENT.
OH, COME ON! DON'T BE A DRAMA QUEEN!
BETTER?
YEAH...
...MY EGO WILL TAKE A BIT LONGER TO RECOVER THOUGH...UGH.
OH, COME ON! YOU GOT A CRAMP DOING SOMETHING STUPID.
YEAH. YOU DIDN'T.
I DO YOGA!
LA-DEE DAH, I DO YOGA!
HEY, COME ON, DON'T BE LIKE THAT.
IT'S MY FAULT FOR TRYING SOMETHING I ONLY EVER SAW IN PORN.
I WANTED TO IMPRESS YOU, YOU KNOW!
WHY?
WELL, YOU'RE CUTE, FUNNY, SEXY... AND I WANT TO KEEP YOU ALL TO MYSELF.
HEH.
AND IF NOTHING ELSE, WE CAN TAKE THIS AS A TEACHING MOMENT.
WHAT'S THE LESSON? ARTISTS ARE INFLEXIBLE CREATURES THAT STRAIN EASILY?

NO.
THE LESSON IS PORN MAKES FOR A PISS-POOR REPLACEMENT FOR A PROPER SEX ED.
I MEAN, THIS LESBIAN THING DOESN'T COME WITH A MANUAL ATTACHED TO IT, SO WHAT DO YOU SAY WE DO THINGS IN OUR OWN WAY AND AT OUR OWN PACE?
HEH, I'D LOVE THAT.
GOOD. NOW RELAX YOUR OLD, FRAGILE BONES, GRANNY MARIANNE, AND LET ME FINISH YOU OFF!
FUCK YOU!

ANYHOW, LONG STORY SHORT, YOU AND I ARE SIGNING UP FOR YOGA TOMORROW!
ALSO, HEY, TOM!
HEY, SORRY I'M LATE, COULDN'T FIND THE PLACE.
OH, HEY.
UH...SO HOW WAS--
THE MODELING?
I WAS GONNA SAY YOUR DAY.
SURE YOU WERE.
WOW, IMMEDIATELY?
FINE!
MY DAY WAS JUST FINE TILL YOU DROPPED IN!
OH MY GOD! YOU TOLD ME TO MEET YOU HERE!

YOU REALLY DID THO--
I...SHUT UP!
I WANTED YOU TO TELL HIM THAT THERE'S NOTHING GOING ON DURING YOUR ART CLASSES.
OH GOD...
HEY, TOM, LISTEN, YOU DON'T HAVE TO WORRY ABOUT SHIT. WE GOT FIVE GUYS THERE AND THEY'RE ALL HYPER-POLITE TO OUR FEMALE MODELS. HONESTLY, THE MOST THEY DO IS AVOID EYE CONTACT AND NOD AT THEM EMBARRASSEDLY WHEN THEY SEE THEM APPROACH.
SEE!?
NOW THE GIRLS ARE A DIFFERENT MATTER ALTOGETHER. WE GOT THIS GOOD-LOOKING DUDE MODELING AS WELL, AND I'M TELLING YOU, YOU WANT TO WEAR RUBBER-SOLED BOOTS CAUSE THE FLOOR IS SLIPPERY WHAT WITH THEM ABSOLUTELY SALIVATING.
IN FACT...YOU SHOULD MODEL FOR US AS WELL
WHAT?!

I'M SAYING, GET SOME BUTT-NAKED METAL GOODNESS IN THAT ROOM, REALLY SPIN SOME HEADS!
HEY!
WHAT? IT'S A PROFESSIONAL ENVIRONMENT! AND YOU CAN COME AND WATCH TOO.
OOOH, A COUPLE NUDE!!! YEAH! BOTH OF YOU POSING TOGETHER!
YEAH...I COULDN'T DO THAT.
OH, COME ON! IT'S PERFECT! YOU GET TO SEE FOR YOURSELF THAT IT'S NO BIG DEAL, AND I GET TO TEASE BOTH OF YOU! SO, WIN/WIN!
NO, I MEAN... WELL...IF I WAS TO BE NAKED WITH HER...I'D HAVE A PROBLEM.
AAAH.
TELL ME MORE ABOUT THIS PROBLEM, BUT FIRST I GOTTA GO TO THE BATHROOM AND THEN I'LL ORDER US SOME GINGER ALE! YOU LIKE GINGER ALE, TOM?
SURE, I LIKE GINGER ALE!
?
PFFF!
YEAH...I BET YOU DO.

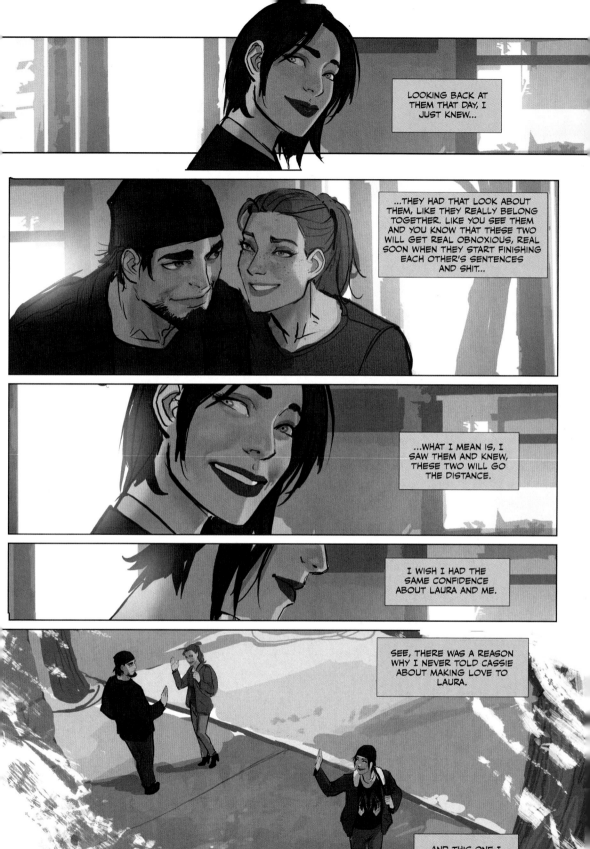

LOOKING BACK AT THEM THAT DAY, I JUST KNEW...

...THEY HAD THAT LOOK ABOUT THEM, LIKE THEY REALLY BELONG TOGETHER. LIKE YOU SEE THEM AND YOU KNOW THAT THESE TWO WILL GET REAL OBNOXIOUS, REAL SOON WHEN THEY START FINISHING EACH OTHER'S SENTENCES AND SHIT...

...WHAT I MEAN IS, I SAW THEM AND KNEW, THESE TWO WILL GO THE DISTANCE.

I WISH I HAD THE SAME CONFIDENCE ABOUT LAURA AND ME.

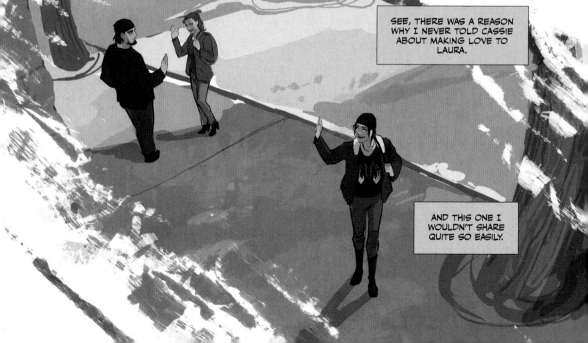

SEE, THERE WAS A REASON WHY I NEVER TOLD CASSIE ABOUT MAKING LOVE TO LAURA.

AND THIS ONE I WOULDN'T SHARE QUITE SO EASILY.

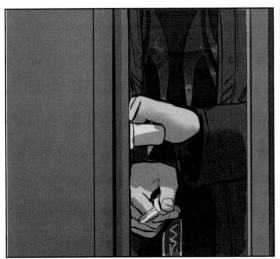
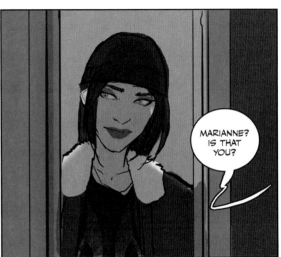

MARIANNE? IS THAT YOU?

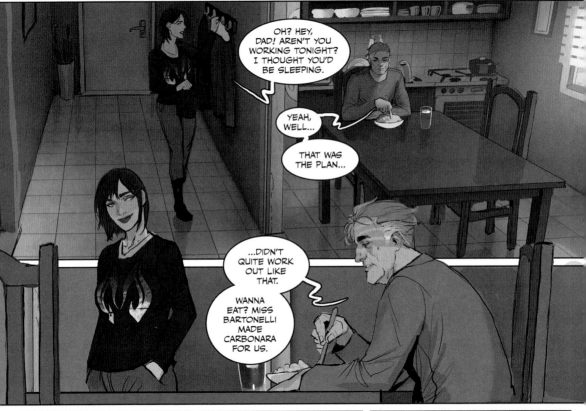

OH? HEY, DAD! AREN'T YOU WORKING TONIGHT? I THOUGHT YOU'D BE SLEEPING.

YEAH, WELL...

THAT WAS THE PLAN...

...DIDN'T QUITE WORK OUT LIKE THAT.

WANNA EAT? MISS BARTONELLI MADE CARBONARA FOR US.

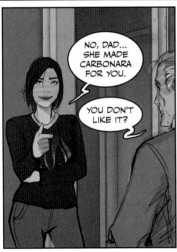

NO, DAD... SHE MADE CARBONARA FOR YOU.

YOU DON'T LIKE IT?

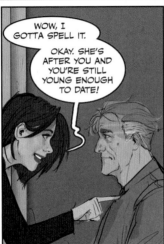

WOW, I GOTTA SPELL IT.

OKAY. SHE'S AFTER YOU AND YOU'RE STILL YOUNG ENOUGH TO DATE!

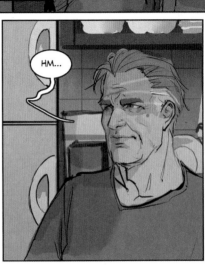

HM...

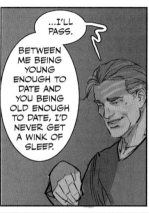

...I'LL PASS.

BETWEEN ME BEING YOUNG ENOUGH TO DATE AND YOU BEING OLD ENOUGH TO DATE, I'D NEVER GET A WINK OF SLEEP.

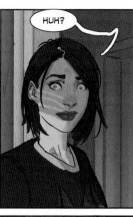

HUH?

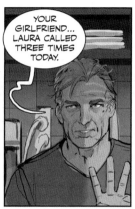

YOUR GIRLFRIEND... LAURA CALLED THREE TIMES TODAY.

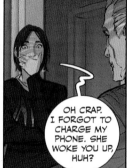

OH CRAP. I FORGOT TO CHARGE MY PHONE. SHE WOKE YOU UP, HUH?

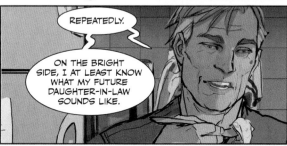

REPEATEDLY.

ON THE BRIGHT SIDE, I AT LEAST KNOW WHAT MY FUTURE DAUGHTER-IN-LAW SOUNDS LIKE.

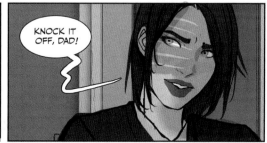

KNOCK IT OFF, DAD!

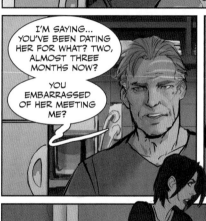

I'M SAYING... YOU'VE BEEN DATING HER FOR WHAT? TWO, ALMOST THREE MONTHS NOW?

YOU EMBARRASSED OF HER MEETING ME?

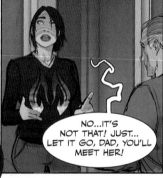

NO...IT'S NOT THAT! JUST... LET IT GO, DAD, YOU'LL MEET HER!

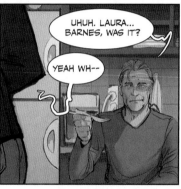

UHUH. LAURA... BARNES, WAS IT?

YEAH WH--

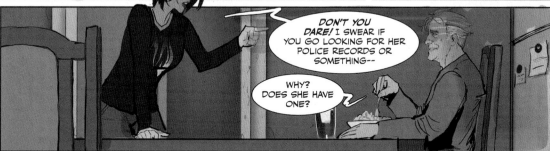

DON'T YOU DARE! I SWEAR IF YOU GO LOOKING FOR HER POLICE RECORDS OR SOMETHING--

WHY? DOES SHE HAVE ONE?

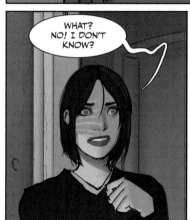

WHAT? NO! I DON'T KNOW?

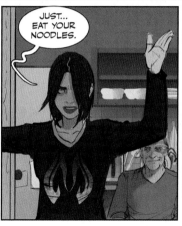

JUST... EAT YOUR NOODLES.

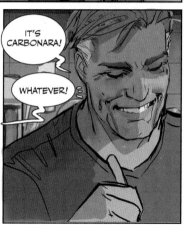

IT'S CARBONARA!

WHATEVER!

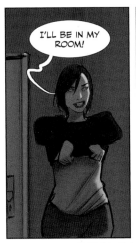

I'LL BE IN MY ROOM!

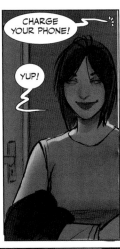

CHARGE YOUR PHONE!

YUP!

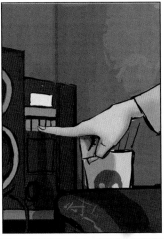

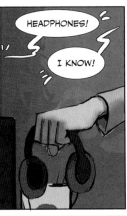

HEADPHONES!

I KNOW!

OF COURSE I WAS GONNA USE HEADPHONES. THAT DAY MORE THAN ANY OTHER, I SOUGHT REFUGE IN THE LYRICS.

I WANTED TO ESCAPE MY OWN THOUGHTS, AFTER ALL...

...AND FOR A WHILE, IT WORKED. AFTER THAT... WELL, THOUGHTS ARE *PERSISTENT* BEASTS.

THEY WILL ALWAYS CATCH UP WITH YOU.

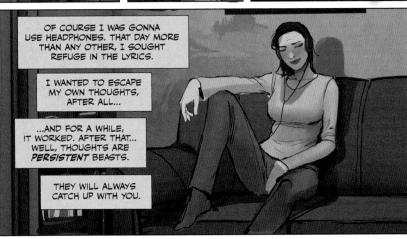

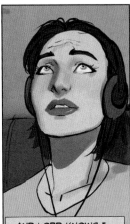

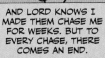

AND LORD KNOWS I MADE THEM CHASE ME FOR WEEKS. BUT TO EVERY CHASE, THERE COMES AN END.

LIKE I SAID, THERE WAS A REASON I NEVER TOLD CASSIE ABOUT MAKING LOVE TO LAURA.

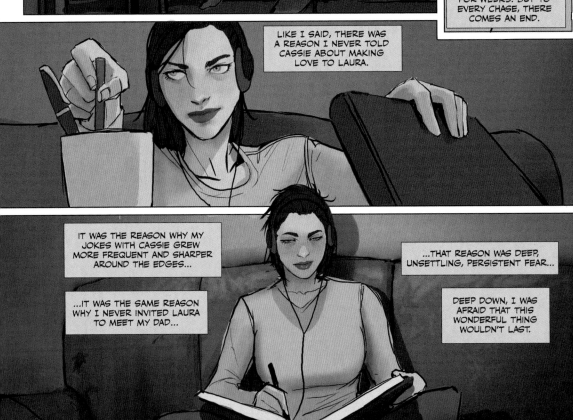

IT WAS THE REASON WHY MY JOKES WITH CASSIE GREW MORE FREQUENT AND SHARPER AROUND THE EDGES...

...IT WAS THE SAME REASON WHY I NEVER INVITED LAURA TO MEET MY DAD...

...THAT REASON WAS DEEP, UNSETTLING, PERSISTENT FEAR...

DEEP DOWN, I WAS AFRAID THAT THIS WONDERFUL THING WOULDN'T LAST.

SEE, WHEN I FIRST MET LAURA, IN MY EYES SHE WAS JUST ANOTHER METALHEAD. JUST A FELLOW FAN OF A BAND. WE HAD STUFF IN COMMON, SHE CAUGHT MY ATTENTION, AND I CONSIDERED ACTING ON MY RECENTLY DISCOVERED SEXUALITY BY GIVING IT...A TEST RUN.

AND AT FIRST, IT WAS GREAT. WE WERE JUST TWO GIRLS HAVING FUN. TWO GIRLS FALLING IN LOVE...

...BUT THEN I GOT TO KNOW HER. AND THE MORE I KNEW ABOUT HER, THE MORE I SAW THIS CONSTANTLY WIDENING GAP FORMING BETWEEN US. SHE WAS THREE YEARS OLDER. SHE HAD HER OWN APARTMENT AND A COOL JOB. SHE HAD FAILED LONG-TERM RELATIONSHIPS AND A BIKE. SHE LIKED SUSHI, AND DID YOGA...SHE HAD HER LIFE FIGURED OUT.

I DIDN'T.

I WAS NINETEEN. I HAD NO IDEA WHAT I WANTED TO BE IN LIFE. I LIVED WITH MY DAD. I HAD SOME ARTISTIC SKILL, AND I COULD MAKE MONEY WITH IT EVERY NOW AND THEN, BUT THAT WAS ABOUT IT. I HAD NO...PLANS.

MY LIFE WAS THE GREAT UNKNOWN.

IT ALL CAME DOWN TO THIS: LAURA WAS AN ADULT.
AND ME? I WAS...HOW DID SHE PUT IT? A KID WEARING HER MOTHER'S CLOTHES? IT WAS AN UNINTENTIONALLY HURTFUL JOKE... BUT SOME OF IT RANG TRUE.
BEER
BEER
I.D.
AFTER ALL, MY WHOLE SELF-IMAGE FELT DEFINED BY A MEMORY OF A BARTENDER REFUSING TO SELL ME BEER.
THAT WAS THE TRUTH OF IT. THE MORE I KNEW ABOUT LAURA, THE MORE I FELT LIKE SOME KID PRETENDING TO BE A GROWN-UP.
CONSTANTLY TRYING TO CATCH UP...
...AND CONSTANTLY FALLING BEHIND.
AND THE FRUSTRATING PART OF IT WAS, IN THEORY, THE SOLUTION TO MY PROBLEM WAS SIMPLE.
IN ORDER FOR THIS RELATIONSHIP TO WORK, I SIMPLY HAD TO GROW UP. GET SERIOUS AND JUST PUT MY BEST FOOT FORWARD.
PROBLEM WAS, THE LAST TIME I TRIED PUTTING MY BEST FOOT FORWARD, THE DAMNED THING CRAMPED UP ON ME.
MURPHY'S LAW, I GUESS.

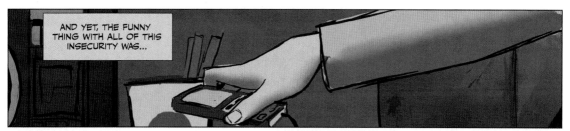

AND YET, THE FUNNY THING WITH ALL OF THIS INSECURITY WAS...

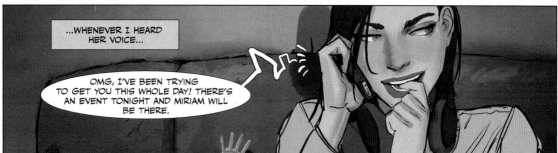

...WHENEVER I HEARD HER VOICE...

OMG, I'VE BEEN TRYING TO GET YOU THIS WHOLE DAY! THERE'S AN EVENT TONIGHT AND MIRIAM WILL BE THERE.

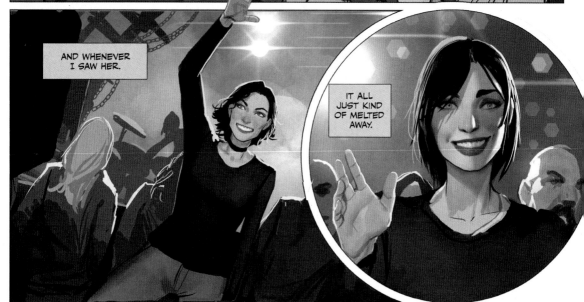

AND WHENEVER I SAW HER.

IT ALL JUST KIND OF MELTED AWAY.

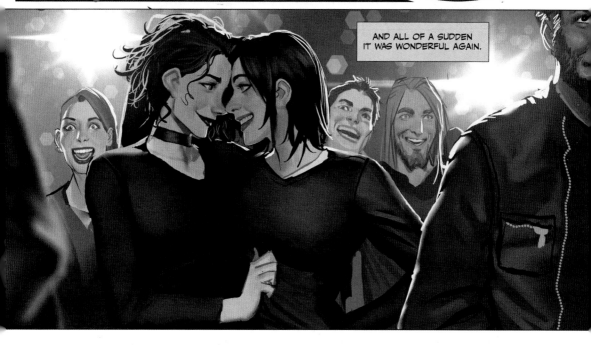

AND ALL OF A SUDDEN IT WAS WONDERFUL AGAIN.

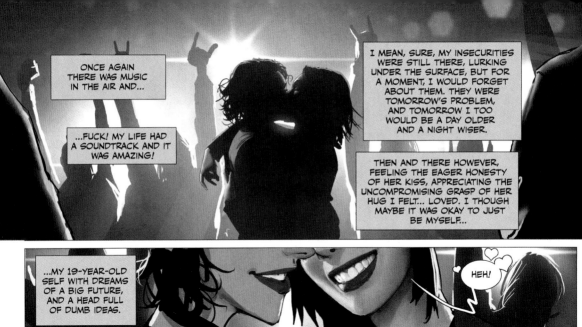

ONCE AGAIN THERE WAS MUSIC IN THE AIR AND...

...FUCK! MY LIFE HAD A SOUNDTRACK AND IT WAS AMAZING!

I MEAN, SURE, MY INSECURITIES WERE STILL THERE, LURKING UNDER THE SURFACE, BUT FOR A MOMENT, I WOULD FORGET ABOUT THEM. THEY WERE TOMORROW'S PROBLEM, AND TOMORROW I TOO WOULD BE A DAY OLDER AND A NIGHT WISER.

THEN AND THERE HOWEVER, FEELING THE EAGER HONESTY OF HER KISS, APPRECIATING THE UNCOMPROMISING GRASP OF HER HUG I FELT... LOVED. I THOUGH MAYBE IT WAS OKAY TO JUST BE MYSELF...

...MY 19-YEAR-OLD SELF WITH DREAMS OF A BIG FUTURE, AND A HEAD FULL OF DUMB IDEAS.

HEH!

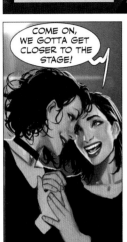

COME ON, WE GOTTA GET CLOSER TO THE STAGE!

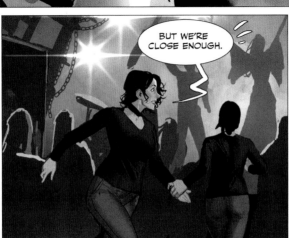

BUT WE'RE CLOSE ENOUGH.

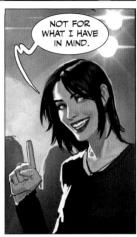

NOT FOR WHAT I HAVE IN MIND.

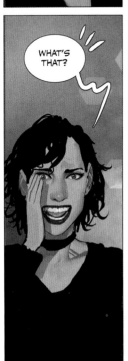

WHAT'S THAT?

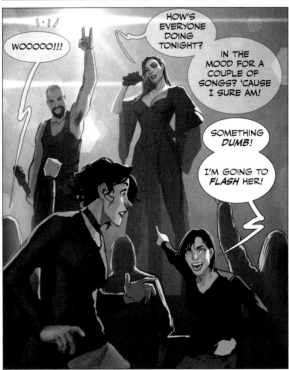

WOOOOO!!!

HOW'S EVERYONE DOING TONIGHT?

IN THE MOOD FOR A COUPLE OF SONGS? 'CAUSE I SURE AM!

SOMETHING *DUMB!*

I'M GOING TO *FLASH* HER!

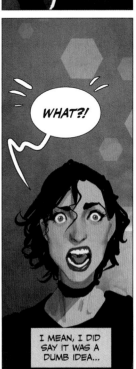

WHAT?!

I MEAN, I DID SAY IT WAS A DUMB IDEA...

BUT...THE THING WITH DUMB IDEAS IS, EVERY NOW AND, THEN THEY MAKE FOR SOME *AMAZING* MEMORIES!
MIRIAAAAM!!!
STOOOP!
HI! MY NAME IS MARIANNE!
WHAT?
I...
...I THOUGHT YOU WERE GONNA SHOW HER YOUR TITS!
HEY! MARIANNE!
I GOT A SONG FOR YOU!

MARIANNE, OF MY DARK HEART...
HOLY CRAP!
...I REMEMBER THE TIME WHEN WE HOWLED AT THE NIGHT.
THE NIGHTS HAVE GROWN COLDER. MY SORROW FEELS OLDER.
THE PAIN OF THIS VOID IN MY SOUL.
EVER SINCE YOU WERE TAKEN MY COURAGE WAS SHAKEN.
MY HEART'S BROKEN PIECES ONCE WHOLE--
COME ON, NOW! ALL TOGETHER!
TO THE MOON I'M CALLING.
MARIANNE OF MY DARK HEART!!!
MY NAME IS MARIANNE

NOW YOU'RE GONE, AND IT'S TEARING ME APART...
WE COULD NEVER IMAGINE LOSING TO THE MORNING LIIIIGHT!
LIKE I SAID...
...SOMETIMES DUMB IDEAS RESULT IN AMAZING MEMORIES.
FLASHING MY FAVORITE SINGER LIKE AN ABSOLUTE IDIOT?
DUMB!

BUT THE MEMORIES... SO FUCKING WORTH IT.
OKAY!
SO MIRIAM JUST TOUCHED MY HAND AND SANG ME A SONG.
KINDA WEIRD TO HAVE YOUR LIFE PEAK AT NINETEEN BUT HERE WE ARE.
ALSO, I HOPE YOU'RE OKAY WITH ME NEVER WASHING THIS HAND AGAIN!!!
HEY! IF YOU WANT THAT HAND TO TOUCH ME AGAIN, YOU BETTER BELIEVE YOU'RE FUCKING WASHING IT.
OOOR, AND HEAR ME OUT HERE, PLAN B!
I COULD JUST GO DOWN ON YOU.
TEMPTING... BUT YOU'RE FREAKISHLY GOOD WITH YOUR HANDS.
WASH IT!
GROAN
FIIIINE! I'LL WASH MY HAND...BUT ONLY BECAUSE YOU MEAN MORE TO ME!

WOOOO!!!! SUCK IT, MIRIAM! I MEAN MORE TO HER!
ALSO, STILL LOVE YOU, BUT I LOVE HER MORE!
HEY, LAURA! I GOT ANOTHER IDEA.
OH!?
UM... OKAY?

COME TO MY PLACE, SHE SAID!
MY DAD'S WORKING, SHE SAID!
CLOTHES ENTIRELY OPTIONAL, SHE SAID!
HEY!
I WASN'T LYING!

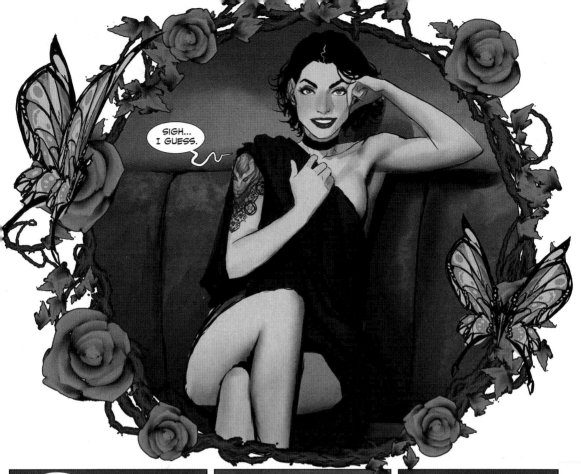

SIGH... I GUESS.

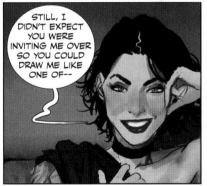

STILL, I DIDN'T EXPECT YOU WERE INVITING ME OVER SO YOU COULD DRAW ME LIKE ONE OF--

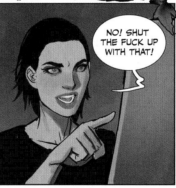

NO! SHUT THE FUCK UP WITH THAT!

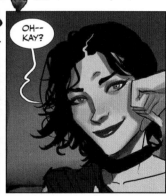

OH-- KAY?

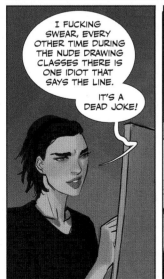

I FUCKING SWEAR, EVERY OTHER TIME DURING THE NUDE DRAWING CLASSES THERE IS ONE IDIOT THAT SAYS THE LINE.

IT'S A DEAD JOKE!

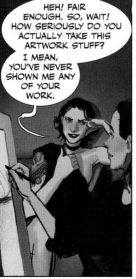

HEH! FAIR ENOUGH. SO, WAIT! HOW SERIOUSLY DO YOU ACTUALLY TAKE THIS ARTWORK STUFF? I MEAN, YOU'VE NEVER SHOWN ME ANY OF YOUR WORK.

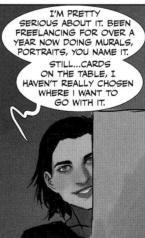

I'M PRETTY SERIOUS ABOUT IT. BEEN FREELANCING FOR OVER A YEAR NOW DOING MURALS, PORTRAITS, YOU NAME IT. STILL...CARDS ON THE TABLE, I HAVEN'T REALLY CHOSEN WHERE I WANT TO GO WITH IT.

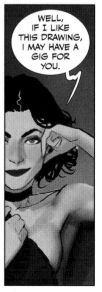

WELL, IF I LIKE THIS DRAWING, I MAY HAVE A GIG FOR YOU.

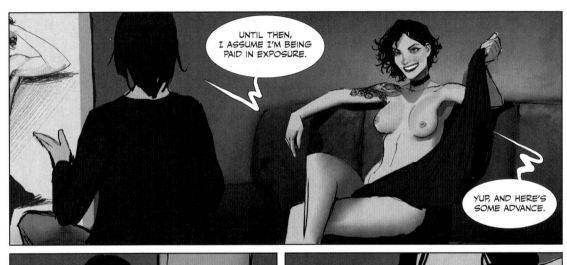

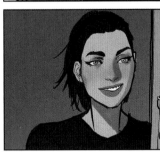

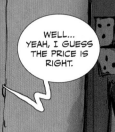

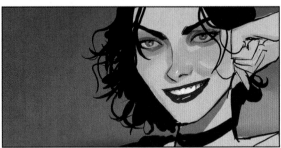

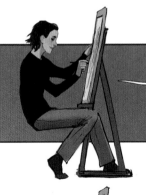

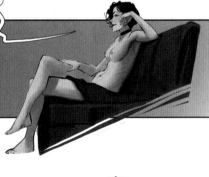

I REMEMBER
THE SILENCE OF
THAT MOMENT.

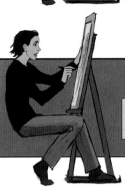

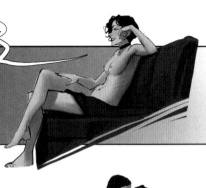

NOT THE SILENCE IN
THE ROOM OR ANYTHING
LIKE THAT.

NO, THIS WAS AN
INNER SILENCE.

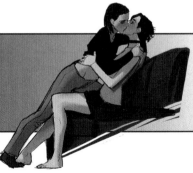

IT WASN'T SOME SPUR-OF-THE-MOMENT JOKE THING SHE SHOUTED AT THE CONCERT. THERE WAS AN ABSOLUTE SIMPLICITY IN THE WAY SHE SAID IT. SHE SOUNDED SO...CERTAIN, AND WITH ALL OF MY HEART, I BELIEVED HER.

FOR THE FIRST TIME IN OVER A MONTH, THE STRANGE TURMOIL WITHIN ME CALMED DOWN.

THE FEARS AND INSECURITIES OF ME SIMPLY NOT BEING GOOD ENOUGH FOR HER DROWNED BY THAT SIMPLEST OF SENTENCES.

ALL THAT WAS LEFT WAS THAT WONDERFUL SILENCE.

AND YET, IN THAT MOMENT OF BLISS, I COULD SCARCELY IMAGINE THE IMPACT THAT NIGHT WOULD HAVE ON THE REST OF MY LIFE...

SEE, AS IT TURNS OUT, I WAS ONLY SEEING HALF OF THE BIG PICTURE.

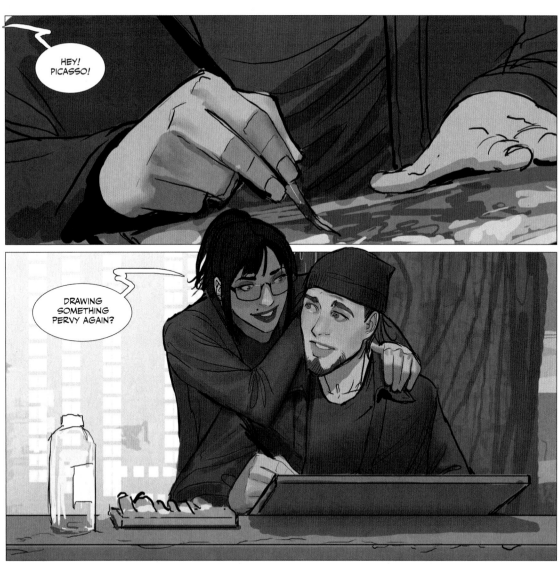

HEY! PICASSO!

DRAWING SOMETHING PERVY AGAIN?

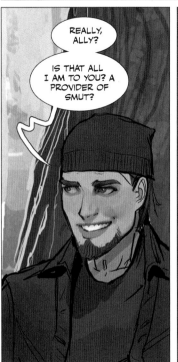

REALLY, ALLY?

IS THAT ALL I AM TO YOU? A PROVIDER OF SMUT?

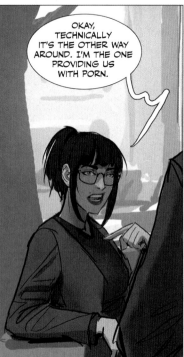

OKAY, TECHNICALLY IT'S THE OTHER WAY AROUND. I'M THE ONE PROVIDING US WITH PORN.

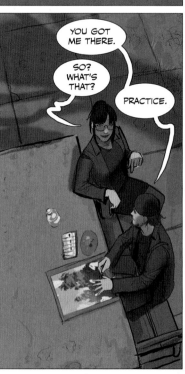

YOU GOT ME THERE.

SO? WHAT'S THAT?

PRACTICE.

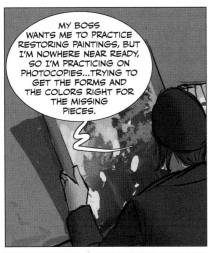

MY BOSS WANTS ME TO PRACTICE RESTORING PAINTINGS, BUT I'M NOWHERE NEAR READY, SO I'M PRACTICING ON PHOTOCOPIES...TRYING TO GET THE FORMS AND THE COLORS RIGHT FOR THE MISSING PIECES.

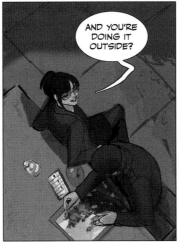

AND YOU'RE DOING IT OUTSIDE?

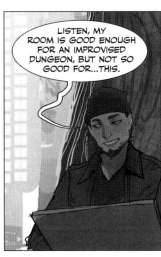

LISTEN, MY ROOM IS GOOD ENOUGH FOR AN IMPROVISED DUNGEON, BUT NOT SO GOOD FOR...THIS.

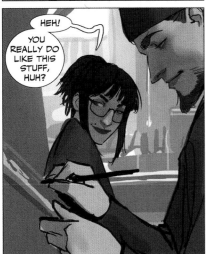

HEH! YOU REALLY DO LIKE THIS STUFF, HUH?

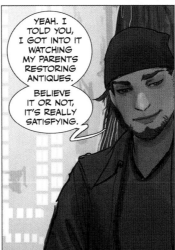

YEAH. I TOLD YOU, I GOT INTO IT WATCHING MY PARENTS RESTORING ANTIQUES.

BELIEVE IT OR NOT, IT'S REALLY SATISFYING.

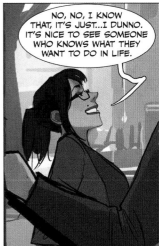

NO, NO, I KNOW THAT, IT'S JUST...I DUNNO. IT'S NICE TO SEE SOMEONE WHO KNOWS WHAT THEY WANT TO DO IN LIFE.

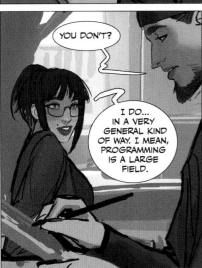

YOU DON'T?

I DO... IN A VERY GENERAL KIND OF WAY. I MEAN, PROGRAMMING IS A LARGE FIELD.

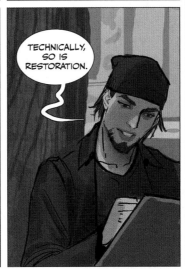

TECHNICALLY, SO IS RESTORATION.

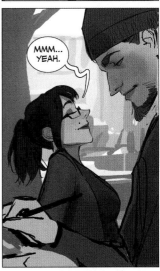

MMM... YEAH.

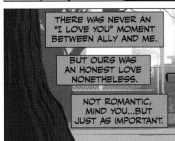

THERE WAS NEVER AN "I LOVE YOU" MOMENT BETWEEN ALLY AND ME.

BUT OURS WAS AN HONEST LOVE NONETHELESS.

NOT ROMANTIC, MIND YOU...BUT JUST AS IMPORTANT.

SHE COULDN'T CARE LESS ABOUT RESTORATION. BUT SHE ALWAYS TOOK THE TIME TO LISTEN TO ME JABBER ON ABOUT THE BEAUTY OF RETURNING SOMETHING TO ITS FORMER GLORY.

I DID THE SAME WHEN SHE TOLD ME OF HER COLLEGE CLASSES ON...HELL, I CAN'T EVEN REMEMBER IT ANYMORE... C PLUS SOMETHING?

AND ANYWAYS, LET'S BE REAL... MOST OF OUR CONVERSATIONS THOSE DAYS WEREN'T ABOUT PROGRAMMING OR RESTORATION.
I ALSO BUILT A LEATHER HARNESS.
AFTER ALL, IT WAS APRIL.
SPRING WAS IN THE AIR.
GO ON?
THAT WONDERFUL TIME OF THE YEAR WHEN A YOUNG COUPLE'S MINDS TURN TO LOVE...

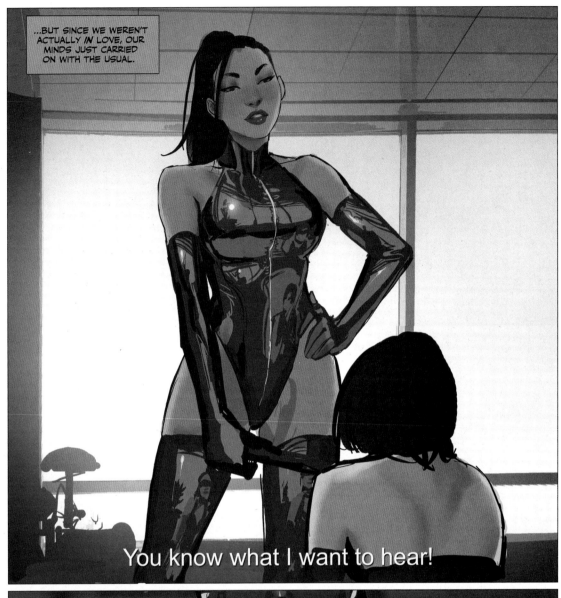

...BUT SINCE WE WEREN'T ACTUALLY *IN* LOVE, OUR MINDS JUST CARRIED ON WITH THE USUAL.

You know what I want to hear!

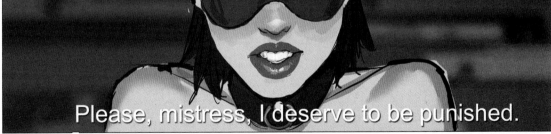

Please, mistress, I deserve to be punished.

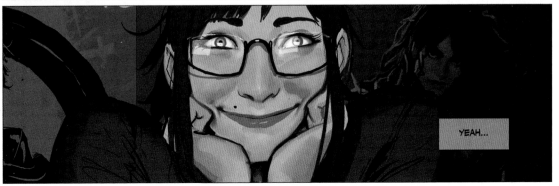

YEAH...

BY THE END OF APRIL, GOING INTO EARLY MAY, WHAT WAS ONCE AN EXCITING THING BECAME A PLEASANT ROUTINE FOR US.
NOT BORING, MIND YOU. NEVER THAT, JUST...COMFORTABLE.
WE WOULD FREQUENTLY SNEAK INTO MY ROOM, BINGE PORN, AND, DEPENDING ON ITS QUALITY, EITHER LAUGH ABOUT IT OR DISCUSS IT IN DETAIL.
MIND YOU, GIVEN HOW FUCKING LOUD WE GOT AT TIMES, I WAS VERY GRATEFUL THAT BOTH ROOMS NEXT TO MINE WERE VACANT.
NOW, GOING BACK TO WHAT ANNE SAID ABOUT LAURA, YOU KNOW, HOW SHE SAID THAT PORN MAKES FOR A PISS-POOR REPLACEMENT FOR SEX ED...
...I'M INCLINED TO AGREE WITH THAT...HOWEVER, THERE'S NO DENYING THE FACT THAT IT OFTEN GAVE ALLY AND ME IDEAS.
I MEAN, IT'S NOT REALLY SOMETHING PEOPLE JUST SLIP INTO CONVERSATIONS THAT EASILY, I GUESS.
OKAY, I'VE NEVER EVEN TRIED MASTURBATING WITH A SHOWERHEAD. LIKE? IS THAT EVEN A THING? WHY DID NOBODY TELL ME THAT WAS A THING?
HI, JANET! HOW'S FAMILY? SAY, I JUST GOT THIS NEW SHOWERHEAD AND I DON'T KNOW WHAT SQUIRTS HARDER, IT OR ME!
CUTE... WANNA TRY IT?
HEY, YOU'RE THE ONE THAT HAS TO SAY YES TO THIS ONE.

READY?
IT'S A SHOWERHEAD, ALAN, NOT A POWER TOOL. I DON'T THINK I HAVE TO BE READY FOR THIS.
FINE. HERE GOES.
MMMH!
WATER PRESSURE SURE IS SHIT HERE, HUH?
SO, WHAT? NOTHING?
I MEAN, IT'S NOT NOTHING, BUT... I DON'T KNOW, MAYBE IT'S THE SHOWERHEAD ITSELF OR, LIKE I SAID, PRESSURE... BUT RIGHT NOW IT FEELS KINDA LIKE I'M BLOWING A RASPBERRY DOWN THERE, BUT LIKE...HALF THE FUN.
OKAY, NOT ALL OF OUR IDEAS WERE WINNERS, BUT WE KEPT TRYING.

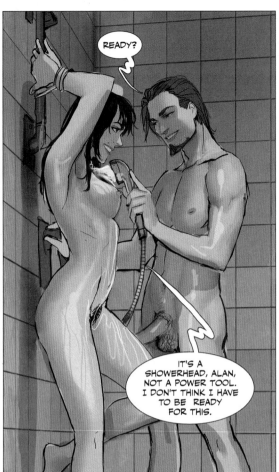

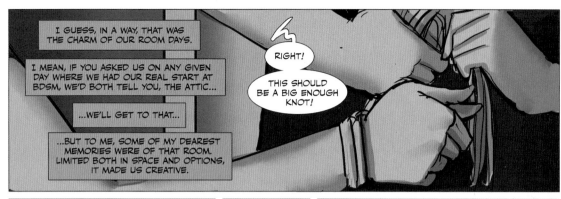

I GUESS, IN A WAY, THAT WAS THE CHARM OF OUR ROOM DAYS.

I MEAN, IF YOU ASKED US ON ANY GIVEN DAY WHERE WE HAD OUR REAL START AT BDSM, WE'D BOTH TELL YOU, THE ATTIC...

...WE'LL GET TO THAT...

...BUT TO ME, SOME OF MY DEAREST MEMORIES WERE OF THAT ROOM. LIMITED BOTH IN SPACE AND OPTIONS, IT MADE US CREATIVE.

RIGHT!

THIS SHOULD BE A BIG ENOUGH KNOT!

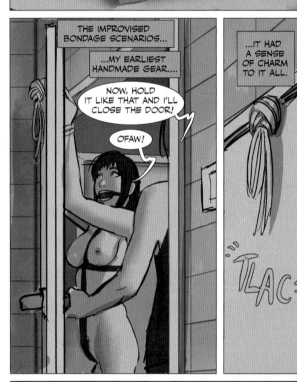

THE IMPROVISED BONDAGE SCENARIOS...

....MY EARLIEST HANDMADE GEAR....

NOW, HOLD IT LIKE THAT AND I'LL CLOSE THE DOOR!

OFAW!

...IT HAD A SENSE OF CHARM TO IT ALL.

TLAC!

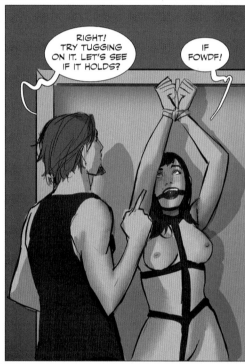

RIGHT! TRY TUGGING ON IT. LET'S SEE IF IT HOLDS?

IF FOWDF!

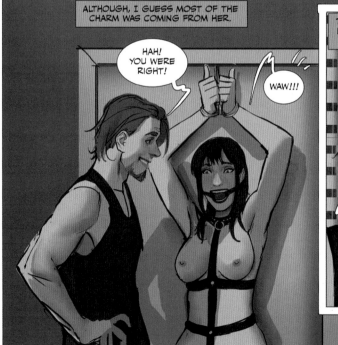

ALTHOUGH, I GUESS MOST OF THE CHARM WAS COMING FROM HER.

HAH! YOU WERE RIGHT!

WAW!!!

THE WHOLE THING WAS LIKE SOME GUERRILLA MAGICIAN'S ACT.

ALLY...

YOU REALLY ARE FUCKING AWESOME.

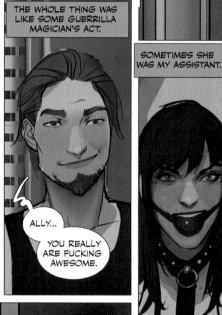

SOMETIMES SHE WAS MY ASSISTANT.

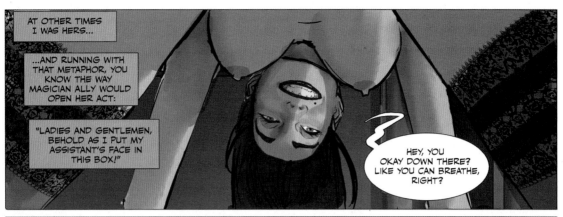

AT OTHER TIMES I WAS HERS...

...AND RUNNING WITH THAT METAPHOR, YOU KNOW THE WAY MAGICIAN ALLY WOULD OPEN HER ACT:

"LADIES AND GENTLEMEN, BEHOLD AS I PUT MY ASSISTANT'S FACE IN THIS BOX!"

HEY, YOU OKAY DOWN THERE? LIKE YOU CAN BREATHE, RIGHT?

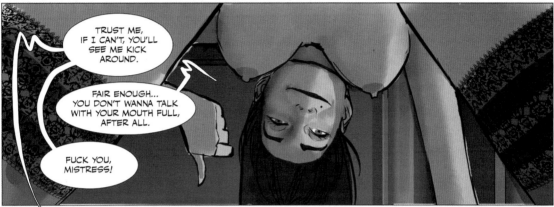

TRUST ME, IF I CAN'T, YOU'LL SEE ME KICK AROUND.

FAIR ENOUGH... YOU DON'T WANNA TALK WITH YOUR MOUTH FULL, AFTER ALL.

FUCK YOU, MISTRESS!

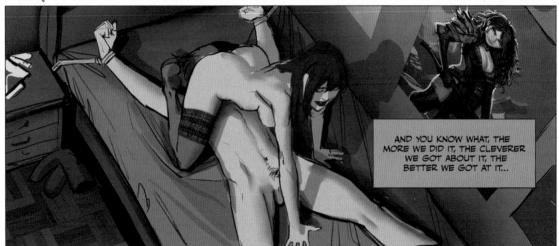

AND YOU KNOW WHAT, THE MORE WE DID IT, THE CLEVERER WE GOT ABOUT IT, THE BETTER WE GOT AT IT...

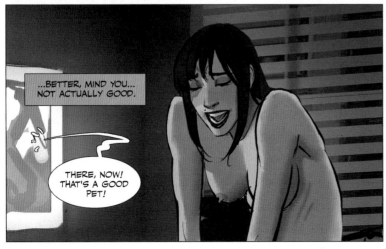

...BETTER, MIND YOU... NOT ACTUALLY GOOD.

THERE, NOW! THAT'S A GOOD PET!

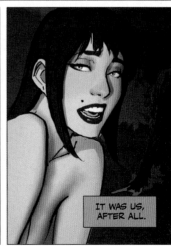

IT WAS US, AFTER ALL.

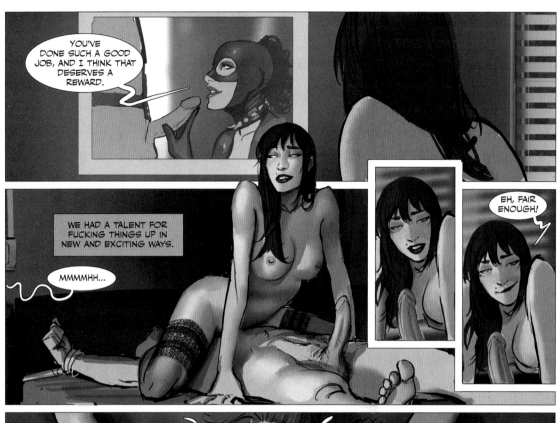

YOU'VE DONE SUCH A GOOD JOB, AND I THINK THAT DESERVES A REWARD.

WE HAD A TALENT FOR FUCKING THINGS UP IN NEW AND EXCITING WAYS.

MMMMHH...

EH, FAIR ENOUGH!

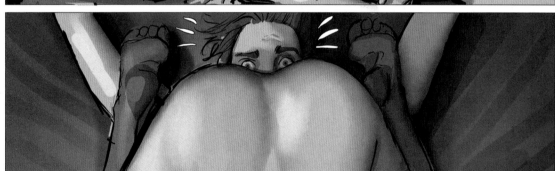

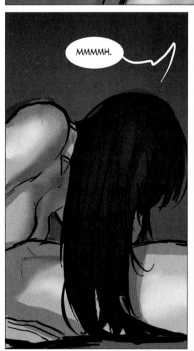

MMMMH.

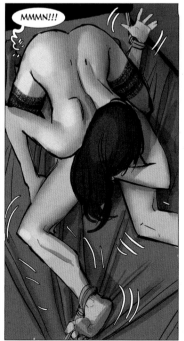

MMMN!!!

PLOP

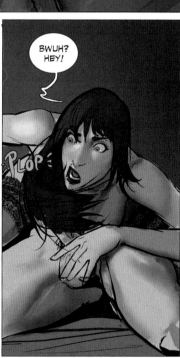

BWUH? HEY!

IT GOT IN MY HAIR!!
I'M SORRY.
ALL OF IT!
I SAID I WAS SORRY!
AND WHAT WAS WITH YOU THRASHING AROUND LIKE THAT. I THOUGHT YOU COULDN'T BREATHE!
HEY! I WAS TRYING TO GET MY DICK OUT OF YOUR MOUTH SO I WOULDN'T...FINISH IN YOUR MOUTH!
I WAS GOING FOR THAT, DAMN IT! I COMMITTED!
OH-- BUT WHY?
I READ PORN STORIES DESCRIBING IT... I MADE A SPLIT-SECOND DECISION...
OKAY?
OH...
YOU COULD HAVE TOLD ME!
YEAH WELL, MY MOUTH WAS KINDA BUSY!
YOU COULD HAVE TOLD ME TO STOP!
YEAH? WELL MY MOUTH WAS KINDA BUSY AS WELL.
PFFFF!!!
BWAHAHAHA!
BUT HEY, I LEARNED SOMETHING! I DON'T LIKE CUMSHOTS!
FUCK OFF!
NO, SERIOUSLY! IT LOOKED LIKE SOMEONE WITH THE WORST COLD IN THE WORLD SNEEZED ALL OVER YOU.
BWAHAHAHH AHAHAH!
MORE SHAMPOO?
YES! BUCKETS OF SHAMPOO PLEASE!

OH FUCK OFF! YOU KNOW HOW MANY TIMES I HAD TO SHAMPOO ALL OF YOUR PUSSY DIP OUT OF MY BEARD? YOU NEVER HEAR ME COMPLAIN!
FIRST OF ALL... YOU CALL THAT A BEARD?
AND SECOND OF ALL...PUSSY... DIP?
WHAT? I DON'T KNOW WHAT TO CALL IT?
PING
THOMP
YEAH...THAT ROOM WAS A PLACE OF MANY DEAR MEMORIES... MANY GOOD THINGS.
BUT AS THE SAYING GOES... ALL GOOD THINGS MUST COME TO AN END.
MMMMH!
DUDE! YOU KICKED IN THE BUTTON TOO HARD, I THINK YOU BUSTED THE ELEVATOR!
HEY! MY HANDS WERE FULL.
FUCK IT, THEN!
ANYWAYS, NOT LIKE ANYONE GIVES A SHIT ABOUT SOME BUSTED ELEVATOR IN THIS DUMP!
SPOILER! THEY GAVE A SHIT.

CAMERAS!?
YEAH...
REMEMBER WHEN YOU WERE LEAVING ON SATURDAY MORNING AND THE ELEVATOR WAS BUSTED SO I SNUCK YOU OUT VIA THE STAIRS?
WELL, TURNS OUT SOME JACKASS KICKED IN THE ELEVATOR BUTTONS, SO THE OWNER DECIDED TO INSTALL CAMERAS ON EVERY FLOOR... HE WAS ALSO KIND ENOUGH TO HIKE OUR RENT TO COVER THE COSTS.
OH COME OOOON!
I EVEN GOT US A FRESH BATCH OF FRIGGIN' PORN FOR TODAY.
I MEAN, I CAN TAKE THOSE OFF YOUR HANDS.
FUCK OFF!
DAMN IT!
YEAH.
SO NOW WHAT?
HONESTLY? NO IDEA.
I GUESS... WE'RE FRIENDS WITH BENEFITS...MINUS THE BENEFITS...

SO, FRIENDS?
I GUESS.
I CAN WORK WITH THAT IF YOU CAN!
I'M GOOD WITH THAT.
SO...NOW THAT OUR PLANS GOT FUCKED... WHAT DO YOU WANNA DO TODAY?
WELL, IF WE CAN'T GO TO YOUR PLACE, I GUESS IT'S HIGH TIME YOU SAW MINE.
HEH! SOUNDS GOOD!
OH...I SHOULD PROOOBABLY MENTION THAT I TOLD MY MOM WE WERE DATING, SOOO...THAT'S A THING.
SO WE'RE LYING TO YOUR MOM--
YOU WANNA TELL HER THE TRUTH?
NOPE!
THERE WE GO, THEN. ANYWAYS, DON'T WORRY. SHE'S A SOFTIE.
YEAH...

...SO ALLY IS A FUCKING LIAR.
RESTORATION?
SO IS THERE GOOD MONEY IN THE RESTORATION BUSINESS?
FAMILY RAISING MONEY? PAYING THE BILLS IN A BAD MONTH MONEY?

I...UM... MUH-MY PARENTS, UH...THEY OWN A SMALL ANTIQUE STORE AND...UH I GUESS NOT EVERY YEAR WAS PERFECT--
SO YOUR IDEA IS TO PIGGYBACK ON YOUR PARENTS' BUSINESS OR...?
I--

HOLY SHIT!
OKAY, I DON'T MEAN TO INTERRUPT, BUT SHE DID THAT SAME SHIT TO ME!
MUNCH MUNCH
LIKE, ALLY WAS ALL LIKE, I'LL INTRODUCE YOU TO MY MOM, COME ON, IT'S GONNA BE FINE!
MUNCH MUNCH
IT WASN'T FINE!
SHE INTRODUCES ME, AND AT FIRST I'M DYING ON THE INSIDE BECAUSE, YOU KNOW...THE WHOLE ME BEING HER DAUGHTER'S LESBIAN GIRLFRIEND THING.
I MEAN, IT WAS A BIT AWKWARD WITH MY MOM AT FIRST, BUT NO...
...ALLY'S MOM? SHE HAS NO INTEREST IN ANY OF THAT...

SO, YOU'RE A WRITER?
ANYTHING OF YOURS PUBLISHED?
I...UH... I'M SHOPPING AROUND FOR AN AGENT.
I SEE...SO UNEMPLOYED.
I MEAN, I'M A PART-TIME WAITRESS.

SO AN UNEMPLOYED WRITER/WAITRESS LIVING WITH MY DAUGHTER...
...I'M SURE YOU PITCH IN ON PAYING THE BILLS REGULARLY THERE.
I--

DAMN... TOUGH MOM!
YEAH, I CAN SEE WHERE ALLY GETS HER DOMME ENERGY FROM.
YOU'RE NOT KIDDING ABOUT HER DOMME ENERGY! WHEN SHE STARTED QUESTIONING ME ABOUT MY WORK, I WAS THIS CLOSE TO ANSWERING WITH YES, MISTRESS!
PFFFF---HACK! COUGH! COUGH!!
AAANYYWAYS, LET'S CONTINUE BEFORE ANNE CHOKES ON HER COOKIE, HERE.
PAT PAT
NONO *KHM* I'M FINE!
SO I'VE BEEN INTERROGATED BY THE POLICE FOUR TIMES IN MY LIFE, ONE OF THEM BEING ANNE'S DAD...AND I FUCKING SWEAR, WITH ALLY'S MOM, THE MOOD WAS THE SAME.
HAVE YOU CONSIDERED THE POSSIBILITY OF YOUR PARENTS' BUSINESS FAILING BY THE TIME YOU'RE READY TO TAKE OVER? WHAT THEN?

JUST LIKE A POLICE DETECTIVE, SHE TOO WAS OUT TO FIND THE TRUTH....
...AND ME? I WAS NEVER GOOD UNDER QUESTIONING.
WELL-- UM...I HAVE BEEN TRYING TO DIVERSIFY MY OPTIONS BY TRYING OUT SOME CRAFTING OF...UH--
NOPE!
MOM! YOU PROMISED YOU WOULDN'T DO THIS!
COME ON, ALAN! I'LL SHOW YOU MY ROOM!
UH-- OKAY.
YOU TWO WANT SOME SNACKS WITH COFFEE?
YES!
THANKS, MOM!
SO...
SO...UH-- WELCOME TO MY ROOM!
USED TO SHARE IT WITH MY SISTER, BUT SHE'S LIVING WITH A COLLEGE ROOMMATE NOW, SO... AT LEAST SOME PRIVACY.

RIGHT...
I DID SAY THAT, DIDN'T I?
UHUH... BUT HEY, REMEMBER HOW YOU WERE ALL LIKE, DON'T WORRY, ALAN! MY MOM'S A BIG SOFTIE?
LISTEN...UH... SHE MEANS WELL, BUT EVER SINCE MY DAD DIED, SHE HAD TO TAKE CARE OF EVERYTHING...WORK TWO JOBS TO KEEP THE BILLS PAID...
OVER TIME SHE'S GOTTEN, UH...PRACTICAL ABOUT LIFE.
SHE DOES MEAN WELL, THO.
FINE...
I'LL TAKE YOUR WORD FOR IT.
GOOD! AND NOW THAT YOU'VE CROSSED THAT GREAT THRESHOLD OF MEETING THE PARENT, YOU'VE EARNED THE RIGHT FOR ME TO SHOW YOU MY DARK SIDE!

TURNS OUT...HER DARK SIDE WAS MORE OF A DORK SIDE.
YOU KNOW... THIS ISN'T HALF BAD.
RIGHT? TOLD YOU IT WAS MY FAVORITE ANIME!
NO, I MEAN US...HERE, LIKE THIS!
LIKE...IT'S US, IN A ROOM TOGETHER, WATCHING STUFF...I DON'T KNOW. IT FEELS FAMILIAR! GOOD FAMILIAR!
I'LL TAKE A POTATO CHIP...
...AND EAT IT!
I REMEMBER SEEING THAT SLIGHT ALLY SMILE ON HER FACE THAT DAY AND THINKING...
YOU HEARD THE MAN!
HEH!
...IT'S STILL THE SAME SMILE... NOTHING FORCED, NOTHING STRANGE ABOUT IT... JUST ALLY BEING ALLY.
WE'LL DO FINE. TURNS OUT...THIS FRIENDSHIP DOESN'T NEED BENEFITS.
AND FOR A WHILE, IT DIDN'T. FOR A WHILE, WE WERE JUST...HAPPY.

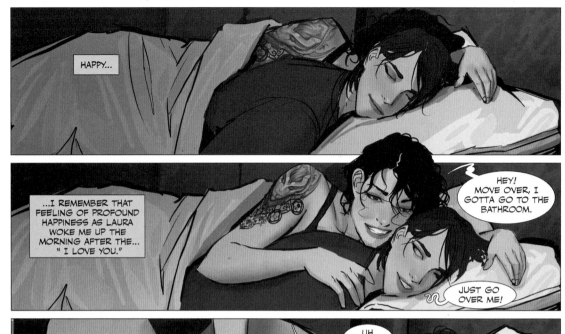

HAPPY...

...I REMEMBER THAT FEELING OF PROFOUND HAPPINESS AS LAURA WOKE ME UP THE MORNING AFTER THE... " I LOVE YOU."

HEY! MOVE OVER, I GOTTA GO TO THE BATHROOM.

JUST GO OVER ME!

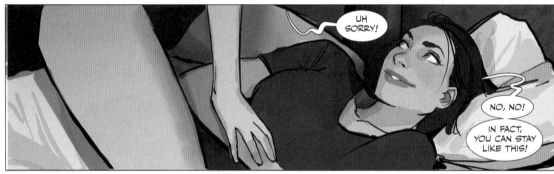

UH SORRY!

NO, NO!

IN FACT, YOU CAN STAY LIKE THIS!

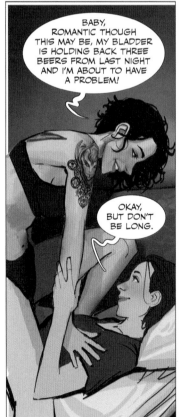

BABY, ROMANTIC THOUGH THIS MAY BE, MY BLADDER IS HOLDING BACK THREE BEERS FROM LAST NIGHT AND I'M ABOUT TO HAVE A PROBLEM!

OKAY, BUT DON'T BE LONG.

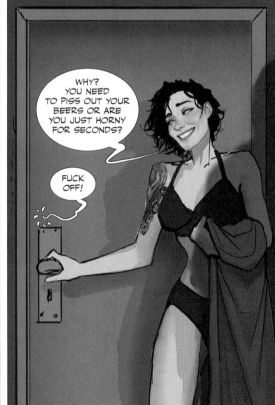

WHY? YOU NEED TO PISS OUT YOUR BEERS OR ARE YOU JUST HORNY FOR SECONDS?

FUCK OFF!

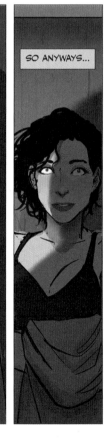

SO ANYWAYS...

...THAT WAS THE MORNING THAT LAURA MET MY DAD.
SO... I'M GUESSING YOU'RE LAURA.
NICE TO FINALLY MATCH THE FACE TO A VERY PERSISTENT VOICE.

MR. MURPHY? I HOPE?

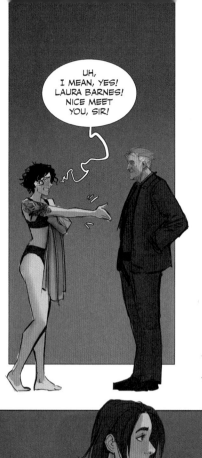

UH, I MEAN, YES! LAURA BARNES! NICE MEET YOU, SIR!

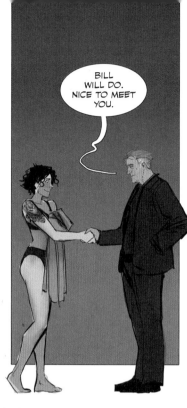

BILL WILL DO. NICE TO MEET YOU.

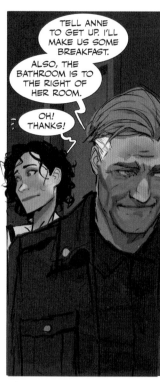

TELL ANNE TO GET UP. I'LL MAKE US SOME BREAKFAST.

ALSO, THE BATHROOM IS TO THE RIGHT OF HER ROOM.

OH! THANKS!

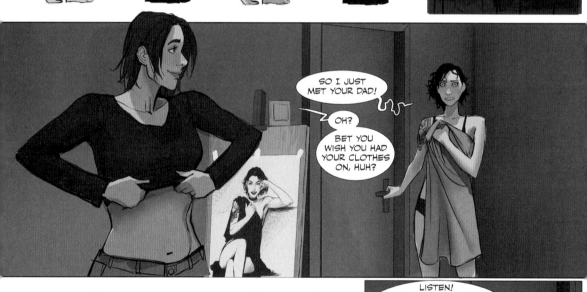

SO I JUST MET YOUR DAD!

OH?

BET YOU WISH YOU HAD YOUR CLOTHES ON, HUH?

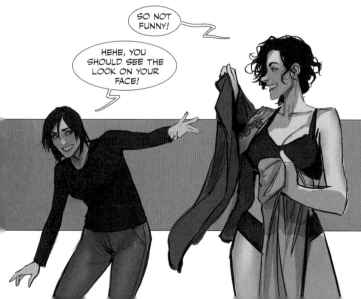

SO NOT FUNNY!

HEHE, YOU SHOULD SEE THE LOOK ON YOUR FACE!

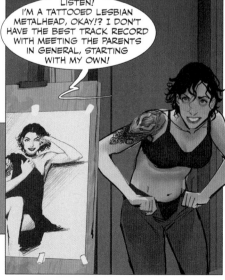

LISTEN! I'M A TATTOOED LESBIAN METALHEAD, OKAY!? I DON'T HAVE THE BEST TRACK RECORD WITH MEETING THE PARENTS IN GENERAL, STARTING WITH MY OWN!

!
HOLD THE PHONE! SO YOU'RE LIKE, ACTUALLY GOOD AT THIS?
I MEAN, I TOLD YOU I'M EARNING MY LIVING THIS WAY.
DID YOU THINK I WAS KIDDING?
NO, IT'S JUST, WHEN PEOPLE TELL YOU, "HEY I CAN DRAW," IT REALLY DOESN'T SAY MUCH. LIKE...OFTEN YOU SEE THEIR WORK AND...
...THEY CAN'T DRAW.
WHAT I MEAN IS, MANAGING A TATTOO PARLOR, I GET PEOPLE COMING AT ME ALL LIKE, "I'M A BIT OF AN ARTIST MYSELF!' MOST OF THE TIME, THEY'RE COMPLETELY DELUSIONAL, SO I JUST NOD POLITELY AND SMILE AT THEM.
LIKE YOU DID TO ME?
OKAY, SO WHEN I SAID I WANTED TO DRAW YOU, YOU WEREN'T REALLY ALL THAT CONFIDENT ABOUT THE OUTCOME, THEN?

I MEAN... I JUST KINDA HOPED THE EVENING WOULD END UP WITH SOME SEX!
WHICH IT DID!
YOU WANT YOUR EGGS SCAMBLED?

UH...SURE...
AND THANK YOU!
BILL?
MHM.
SO YOU KNOW HOW YOU SAID YOU DON'T DO WELL WITH MEETING THE PARENTS? I CAN'T HELP WITH YOURS, BUT AS FOR OTHER PEOPLE'S PARENTS, MAYBE JUST DONT SAY STUPID SHIT OUT LOUD LIKE THAT.
YE--AH.

NOW LET'S GO AND HAVE WHAT WILL PROBABLY BE THE MOST AWKWARD BREAKFAST OF MY LIFE!
OKAY, JUST LEMME GET MY PHONE.
SURE!
HEY, DAD! I'LL HELP YOU WITH THE EGGS!

IT'S FUNNY, YOU KNOW.
IF YOU ASKED ME BACK THEN WHAT I THOUGHT WAS THE MOST LIFE-CHANGING PART OF THAT WEEK...
...I WOULD HAVE ANSWERED: LAURA TELLING ME THOSE THREE WONDERFUL WORDS.
I LOVE YOU.
BELIEVE IT OR NOT, IMPORTANT THOUGH THAT WONDERFUL MOMENT WAS, IT WOULD HAVE BEEN THE WRONG ANSWER.
NO, AS IT TURNED OUT, THE MOST LIFE-DEFINING PART OF THAT WEEK WAS THE DRAWING...
...THE DRAWING THAT GAVE LAURA THE IDEA...

...THAT MADE HER SAY THOSE OTHER THREE LIFE-CHANGING WORDS:
IT'S A SURPRISE!
OKAY, TECHNICALLY MAYBE THAT'S FOUR WORDS. SCREW IT, I'M AN ARTIST, NOT A WRITER.
A SURPRISE...
...YEAH, NO! YOU KNOW WHAT? YOU BURNED THROUGH YOUR YEARLY SURPRISE ALLOWANCE ALREADY!
WH--
WHAT DO YOU MEAN?

YOUR EVERY SINGLE ENCOUNTER WITH MY DAD... WHICH SOMEHOW, TO MY DISBELIEF, ENDED UP EVEN INCLUDING THE BREAKFAST!
OKAY, WHAT WAS WRONG WITH THE BREAKFAST!?
EITHER OF YOU NEED TO USE THE BATHROOM?
ALL GOOD.
ALL YOURS, DAD.
SO, I'M THINKING! THIS SATURDAY, WE GO TO THE THUNDERDOME AND THEN LATER WE GO TO MY PLACE...
I--
...I GOT A COCKTAIL-MIXING SET I AM ITCHING TO TRY OUT AND NEW BEDSHEETS FOR US TO STRESS TEST!
I FORGOT MY NEWSPAPER.
HEY, I CAN'T BE BLAMED FOR HIS SENSE OF TIMING!
IT'S YOUR TIMING!

UH...ON THAT NOTE...I GUESS I DIDN'T LEAVE THE BEST FIRST IMPRESSION, HUH?
IT...COULD HAVE BEEN BETTER.
LATER THAT DAY, I HAD TO HAVE "THE TALK" WITH MY DAD!
AND JUST SO YOU UNDERSTAND, I HAVEN'T HAD TO HAVE "THE TALK" IN YEARS. THIS IS THE MAN THAT WHEN I TOLD HIM I WAS BI, HE ROLLED WITH IT. WHEN I TOLD HIM I WAS SPENDING THE NIGHT AT YOUR PLACE THAT TIME, HE ROLLED WITH IT, BUT AFTER METING YOU...
...THE TALK!
ANNE...
IS SHE ON DRUGS?
NO, DAD... SHE'S JUST... A BIT PARENTALLY AWKWARD.
ANYWAYS, I WORKED IT OUT...
STILL, AT THIS POINT, WHEN YOU TELL ME YOU HAVE A SURPRISE FOR ME...
I'M NOT GONNA LIE, I WORRY A BIT!
THIS TIME IT'S A GOOD SURPRISE!
I PROMISE.
UGH, FINE!

AND YOU KNOW WHAT... IT WAS A GOOD SURPRISE. IN FACT, IT WAS AN AMAZING ONE!
BUT LIKE... EVENTUALLY.
MARIANNE, I'D LIKE TO INTRODUCE YOU TO JACOB JOHNSON! THE BEST TATTOO ARTIST IN THIS SHOP AND I'D SAY BEYOND!
OH, HEY!
BECAUSE THAT FIRST DAY...
'SUP!
AND JACOB, I'D LIKE TO INTRODUCE YOU TO MARIANNE MURPHY! YOUR NEW APPRENTICE!
SAYWHATNOW?
...THINGS COULD HAVE GONE BETTER.
HUH?

HEY, LAURA, THIS ISN'T HOW I DO THINGS.
OH, COME ON, JACOB! YOU ARE THE BEST AND SHE IS JUST...AMAZING! I PROMISE SHE CAN DRAW.
AND SHE LOVES TATTOOS.
HEY, YOU LOVE TATTOOS?
I...UH--I LIKE THEM.
LIKE THEM... UHUH.
LAURA, HOW MANY TIMES HAVE YOU BROUGHT IN SOME FRIEND OF YOURS THAT CAN DRAW AND LIKES TATTOOS?
OF COURSE, THEY ALL END UP WASTING MY TIME BY QUITTING AFTER THEY REALIZE THAT THIS IS NOT JUST ABOUT KNOWING HOW TO DRAW, THAT SKIN ISN'T FUCKING PAPER AND THERE ARE NO EASY DO-OVERS.
WELL?
HOW MANY TIMES HAVE WE DONE THIS SO FAR?
I...
I'LL TELL YOU HOW MANY. FIVE!
...THIS IS DIFFERENT!
YEAH, THIS TIME YOU'RE DATING HER.
HEY FUCK YOU!
NO, FUCK YOU!

LISTEN, NO OFFENSE, KID. I'M SURE YOU CAN DRAW. LAURA HAS AN EYE FOR THAT, BUT SHE'S TERRIBLE AT FINDING ACTUAL TATTOO ARTISTS, AND I'M NOT INTERESTED IN TEACHING SOME DABBLER WHO ISN'T FULLY COMMITTED TO THIS.
WH-WHAT'S HAPPENNING?
OH, COME ON, JACOB...
...YOU'RE KILLING ME, HERE! YOU KNOW THAT?
I GOT SHIT TO DO. DON'T DO THIS AGAIN, LAURA, OR I'M CALLING ANDERSON ON YOU!
SHIT... THIS COULD HAVE GONE BETTER.
UHHHH...
YEAH!
SO THIS IS WHERE I WORK.
SURPRISEEE!

LAURA, WHAT THE FUCK WAS THAT???
OKAY, I'M SORRY!
I...SAW YOUR ART AND I THOUGHT...YOU'D MAKE A BADASS TATTOO ARTIST AND I KINDA WANTED TO MAKE IT A SURPRISE AND--
IT SEEMS THAT WAS KIND OF A BAD IDEA.
YOU THINK?
MAYBE NEXT TIME DON'T PLAN MY LIFE AHEAD OF TIME WITHOUT ME KNOWING ANYTHING ABOUT IT?
I...I'M SORRY.
I'M GOING HOME.
I GOTTA SLEEP OFF THIS EMBARRASSMENT RIGHT NOW.
I...CAN I CALL YOU?
ARGH!
THAT WASN'T A NO?

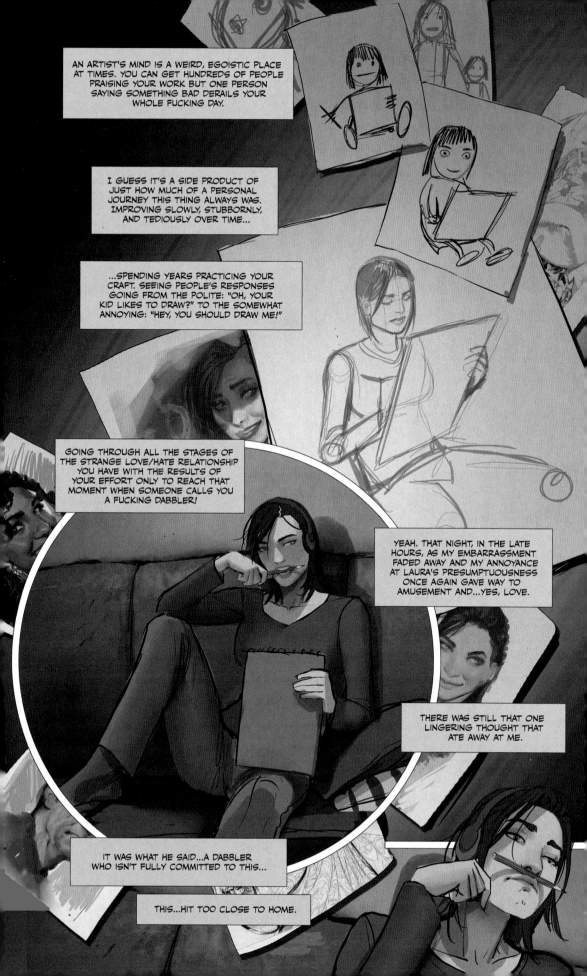

AN ARTIST'S MIND IS A WEIRD, EGOISTIC PLACE AT TIMES. YOU CAN GET HUNDREDS OF PEOPLE PRAISING YOUR WORK BUT ONE PERSON SAYING SOMETHING BAD DERAILS YOUR WHOLE FUCKING DAY.

I GUESS IT'S A SIDE PRODUCT OF JUST HOW MUCH OF A PERSONAL JOURNEY THIS THING ALWAYS WAS. IMPROVING SLOWLY, STUBBORNLY, AND TEDIOUSLY OVER TIME...

...SPENDING YEARS PRACTICING YOUR CRAFT. SEEING PEOPLE'S RESPONSES GOING FROM THE POLITE: "OH, YOUR KID LIKES TO DRAW?" TO THE SOMEWHAT ANNOYING: "HEY, YOU SHOULD DRAW ME!"

GOING THROUGH ALL THE STAGES OF THE STRANGE LOVE/HATE RELATIONSHIP YOU HAVE WITH THE RESULTS OF YOUR EFFORT ONLY TO REACH THAT MOMENT WHEN SOMEONE CALLS YOU A FUCKING DABBLER!

YEAH. THAT NIGHT, IN THE LATE HOURS, AS MY EMBARRASSMENT FADED AWAY AND MY ANNOYANCE AT LAURA'S PRESUMPTUOUSNESS ONCE AGAIN GAVE WAY TO AMUSEMENT AND...YES, LOVE.

THERE WAS STILL THAT ONE LINGERING THOUGHT THAT ATE AWAY AT ME.

IT WAS WHAT HE SAID...A DABBLER WHO ISN'T FULLY COMMITTED TO THIS...

THIS...HIT TOO CLOSE TO HOME.

THIS MUCH WAS TRUE ABOUT ME. I WAS ALWAYS INDECISIVE ABOUT MY INTERESTS, EVEN WITH THIS ONE THING THAT I KNEW HOW TO DO. I NEVER REALLY HAD ANY CLEAR GOALS. WOULD I BE AN ILLUSTRATOR? A PAINTER? A MURALIST? A COMIC ARTIST, PERHAPS? A PRODUCT DESIGNER?
A TATTOO ARTIST?
TRUTH WAS, I HAD NO CLEAR IDEA. THEN AGAIN, THAT WAS ME IN A NUTSHELL. TRYING STUFF OUT.
DANCING, MARTIAL ARTS, SPORTS, AND DIFFERENT CLUBS AND HOBBIES.
ALWAYS STARTING BUT NEVER COMMITTING.
JUST...DABBLING.
HELL...THIS WAS TRUE EVEN FOR SOME OF MY MOST RECENT ESCAPADES.
ANYHOW, LONG STORY SHORT, YOU AND I ARE SIGNING UP FOR YOGA TOMORROW!
SO WE DID YOGA.
OMG, I FEEL SORE BUT LIKE, GOOD SORE, LIKE I FEEL ENERGIZED. WE GOTTA DO THIS AGAIN.
ONCE.
AGAIN BEING WHEN?
I DUNNO.

YEAH...TURNS OUT I REALLY WAS A CHRONICALLY INDECISIVE DABBLER...
SIGH.
THE BIG QUESTION WAS...WHAT WAS I GONNA DO ABOUT IT?
FUCK IT!
DIN-DLINN
JUST GIMME A SEC, I'M IN THE BACK.
HEY WASSU--
OH, IT'S YOU, UH...LAURA IS NOT HERE.
I KNOW. I CALLED HER TO MAKE SURE.
OK?
I...UH... I WANTED TO TALK TO YOU IF THAT'S OKAY? YOU GOT A FEW MINUTES?
SURE. IT'S A SLOW DAY ANYWAYS.
COFFEE?
SURE!

UH...THIS IS ABOUT THE LAST TIME I WAS HERE.
AH.
I GUESS I WANTED TO APOLOGIZE ON BEHALF OF LAURA AND WELL...UH, YOU WERE KINDA RIGHT.
?
YOU CALLED ME A DABBLER.
HEY, DON'T TAKE IT HARD, I WAS IN A BAD M--
NO, THAT'S JUST IT! LIKE I SAID, YOU WERE KINDA RIGHT.
WHEN YOU ASKED ME IF I LOVED TATTOOS, I GAVE YOU THE SAME LEVEL OF ENTHUSIASM AS IF YOU ASKED ME ABOUT ANY OTHER MEDIUM...
...THING IS, I STILL HAVEN'T REALLY PICKED A LANE, YOU KNOW?
BUT YOU *CAN* DRAW?
DRAW, PAINT, TRIED SOME SCULPTING, GRAFFITI, AIRBRUSHING...
HEH...JACK OF ALL, HUH? SO WHERE COULD I HAVE SEEN YOUR WORK, THEN?
WELL... THERE ARE ABOUT A DOZEN OR SO SANDWICH SHOPS OUT THERE WITH MY MURALS ON THEM.
SANDWICH SHOPS?

YEAH. I TOOK A GIG FROM ONE, THEN ANOTHER SHOP OWNER SAW IT AND SAID, "THAT'S A TASTY-ASS LOOKING SANDWICH," AND ASKED FOR MY INFO AND...
...I SOON BECAME THE SANDWICH GIRL...
NOT IN A PERVERTED WAY.
HEH.
ANY OF THEM NEAR?
SIX-ISH BLOCKS FROM HERE? CONNOR'S?
OH, I'VE SEEN THAT ONE.
THAT'S A TASTY-ASS LOOKING SANDWICH.
SO ANYWAYS, I JUST WANTED TO APOLOGIZE. I KNOW LAURA WENT A BIT TOO HARD.
LAURA WILL DO LAURA THINGS, I'M USED TO HER NONSENSE.
SHE MEANS WELL... BUT...SHE JUMPS INTO THINGS WITHOUT THINKING AND FACE-PLANTS TOO OFTEN.
YEAH, YOU MAY BE ONTO SOMETHING THERE.

OKAY, SO NOW THAT WE'VE CLEARED THE AIR A BIT, THERE IS SOMETHING I WANTED TO ASK YOU.
UH, IF IT'S NOT TOO MUCH OF A BOTHER, I'M NOT ASKING FOR AN APPRENTICESHIP, BUT I'D LIKE TO WATCH YOU WORK SOMETIMES...JUST SEE IF THIS IS SOMETHING THAT I MIGHT ACTUALLY BE INTO.
FAIR ENOUGH. MARIANNE, WAS IT?
JUST ANNE IS FINE.
ANNE... ALRIGHT.
LET'S SEE WHAT YOU GOT, SANDWICH GIRL!

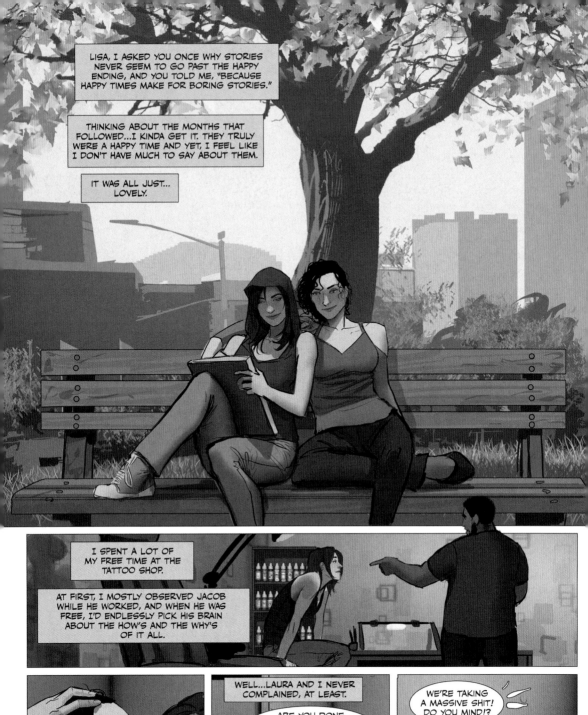

LISA, I ASKED YOU ONCE WHY STORIES NEVER SEEM TO GO PAST THE HAPPY ENDING, AND YOU TOLD ME, "BECAUSE HAPPY TIMES MAKE FOR BORING STORIES."

THINKING ABOUT THE MONTHS THAT FOLLOWED...I KINDA GET IT. THEY TRULY WERE A HAPPY TIME AND YET, I FEEL LIKE I DON'T HAVE MUCH TO SAY ABOUT THEM.

IT WAS ALL JUST... LOVELY.

I SPENT A LOT OF MY FREE TIME AT THE TATTOO SHOP.

AT FIRST, I MOSTLY OBSERVED JACOB WHILE HE WORKED, AND WHEN HE WAS FREE, I'D ENDLESSLY PICK HIS BRAIN ABOUT THE HOW'S AND THE WHY'S OF IT ALL.

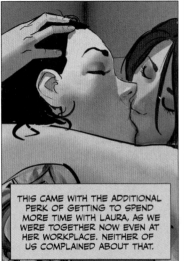

THIS CAME WITH THE ADDITIONAL PERK OF GETTING TO SPEND MORE TIME WITH LAURA, AS WE WERE TOGETHER NOW EVEN AT HER WORKPLACE. NEITHER OF US COMPLAINED ABOUT THAT.

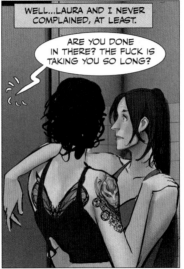

WELL...LAURA AND I NEVER COMPLAINED, AT LEAST.

ARE YOU DONE IN THERE? THE FUCK IS TAKING YOU SO LONG?

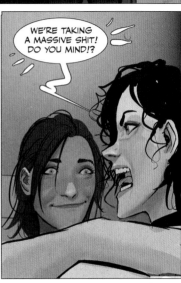

WE'RE TAKING A MASSIVE SHIT! DO YOU MIND!?

AS DAYS TURNED TO WEEKS, I WENT FROM MERELY OBSERVING TO HELPING WITH CLEANING, MAINTENANCE, AND STERILIZATION OF THE GEAR.
AND THE WEIRD THING WAS, THE MORE COMPLICATED THIS WHOLE THING GOT, THE MORE INTRIGUED I WAS BY IT.
IT WAS A STRANGE THING FOR A CHRONIC DABBLER LIKE ME TO GET INVESTED LIKE THAT. BUT FOR THE FIRST TIME EVER, I COULDN'T WAIT TO GET HOME FROM COLLEGE, DROP OFF MY THINGS, AND RUN BACK TO MY HOME AWAY FROM HOME BECAUSE I WANTED TO LEARN MORE!
I GUESS IT HELPED THAT MY TEACHER WAS AS PASSIONATE ABOUT HIS CRAFT AS HE WAS PATIENT WITH ME.
I DUNNO, TRACING TO ME ALWAYS FELT LIKE CHEATING.
IT'S STENCILLING, AND TRUST ME, YOUR CLIENTS WON'T CARE MUCH ABOUT YOUR CREATIVE INTEGRITY ONCE THEY GET A MISALIGNED, WONKY TATTOO ON THEIR SKIN.
EVENTUALLY IT GOT UNDER MY SKIN. SEE, I REALIZED WHAT KEPT ME FROM QUITTING THIS LIKE I QUIT MOST OTHER THINGS. TATTOOING EXISTED ON THIS STRANGE INTERSECTION OF FAMILIAR AND NEW. IT WAS LIKE PICKING UP A FAVORITE TOY AND REALIZING AFTER ALL THAT TIME THERE WERE HIDDEN MECHANISMS IN IT.
NEW WAYS TO PLAY WITH IT.

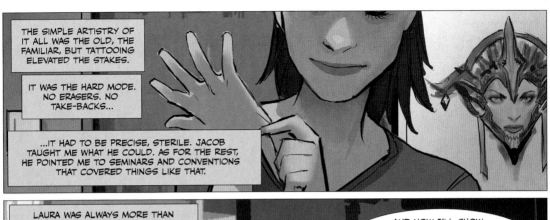

THE SIMPLE ARTISTRY OF IT ALL WAS THE OLD, THE FAMILIAR, BUT TATTOOING ELEVATED THE STAKES.

IT WAS THE HARD MODE. NO ERASERS. NO TAKE-BACKS...

...IT HAD TO BE PRECISE, STERILE. JACOB TAUGHT ME WHAT HE COULD. AS FOR THE REST, HE POINTED ME TO SEMINARS AND CONVENTIONS THAT COVERED THINGS LIKE THAT.

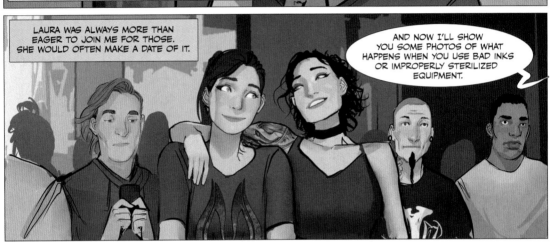

LAURA WAS ALWAYS MORE THAN EAGER TO JOIN ME FOR THOSE. SHE WOULD OFTEN MAKE A DATE OF IT.

AND NOW I'LL SHOW YOU SOME PHOTOS OF WHAT HAPPENS WHEN YOU USE BAD INKS OR IMPROPERLY STERILIZED EQUIPMENT.

AT TIMES, A VERY UNSETTLING DATE.

THE YELLOW STUFF HERE IS INK. THE REST IS PUS.

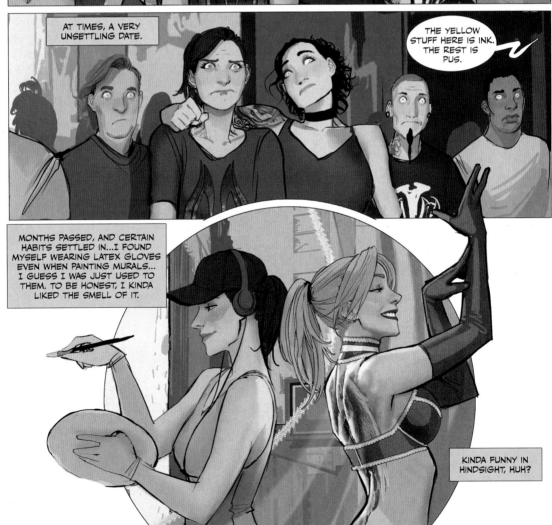

MONTHS PASSED, AND CERTAIN HABITS SETTLED IN...I FOUND MYSELF WEARING LATEX GLOVES EVEN WHEN PAINTING MURALS... I GUESS I WAS JUST USED TO THEM. TO BE HONEST, I KINDA LIKED THE SMELL OF IT.

KINDA FUNNY IN HINDSIGHT, HUH?

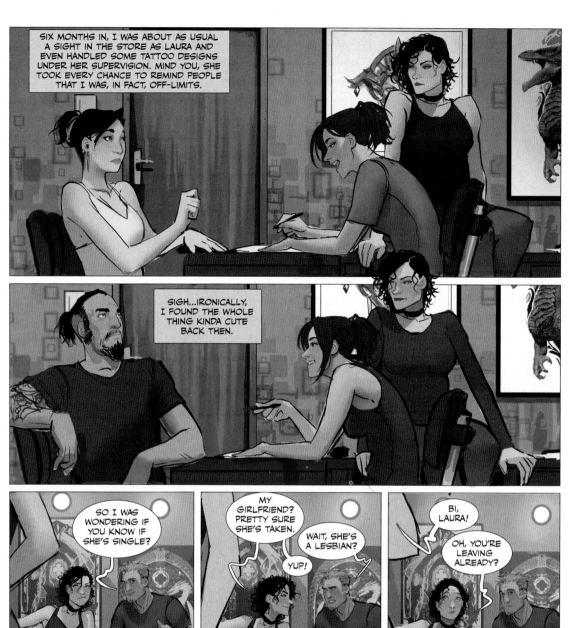

SIX MONTHS IN, I WAS ABOUT AS USUAL A SIGHT IN THE STORE AS LAURA AND EVEN HANDLED SOME TATTOO DESIGNS UNDER HER SUPERVISION. MIND YOU, SHE TOOK EVERY CHANCE TO REMIND PEOPLE THAT I WAS, IN FACT, OFF-LIMITS.

SIGH...IRONICALLY, I FOUND THE WHOLE THING KINDA CUTE BACK THEN.

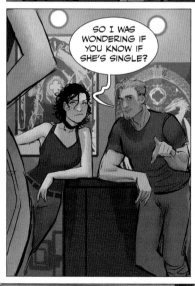

SO I WAS WONDERING IF YOU KNOW IF SHE'S SINGLE?

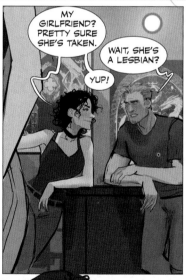

MY GIRLFRIEND? PRETTY SURE SHE'S TAKEN.

WAIT, SHE'S A LESBIAN?

YUP!

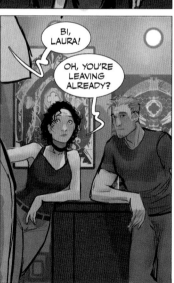

BI, LAURA!

OH, YOU'RE LEAVING ALREADY?

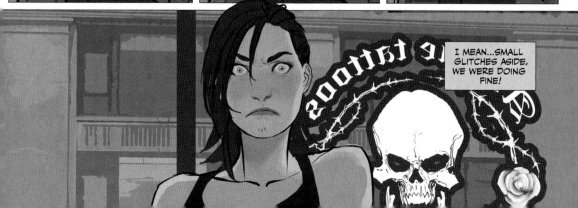

I MEAN...SMALL GLITCHES ASIDE, WE WERE DOING FINE!

NOW, SPEAKING OF THINGS GOING JUST FINE, I SOON GRADUATED MY WAY UP TO TATTOOING FRUIT, GETTING A FEEL FOR THE MACHINE, THE WEIGHT, THE MOVEMENT, SPEED DEPTH...MIND YOU, PRACTICING TATTOOING WAS NOTHING LIKE PRACTICING DRAWING. AFTER ALL, IT WASN'T LIKE YOU COULD JUST PICK UP SOME RANDOM PIECES OF SKIN AND DOODLE ON THEM...
WELL...THAT'S WHAT I THOUGHT BACK THEN.
SO I'VE BEEN MEANING TO ASK, WHAT'S THE BEST THING TO PRACTICE ON?
YOU'RE SURE?
OH YEAH, PIGSKIN ALL THE WAY. DIG IN, GIRL.
I HOOKED YOU UP WITH A BUNCH OF IT. I GOT A GUY! NOW, GET TO IT WHILE IT'S NICE AND FRESH.
OH, SPEAKING OF WHICH, ANYONE UP FOR A PULLED PORK SANDWICH?
DUMB JOKES AND THE GROSS-OUT FACTOR ASIDE, HE WAS RIGHT ABOUT IT. IT FELT LIKE THE REAL DEAL. SO I GOT TO PRACTICING LIKE NEVER BEFORE.
AND YOU KNOW WHAT? SOON ENOUGH, I FELT LIKE THE REAL DEAL.
WELL, I'LL BE DAMNED, THE SANDWICH GIRL RANKED UP TO TATTOO GIRL. THEY GROW UP SO FAST!
I GUESS WE GOTTA FIND YOU A VOLUNTEER TO GRADUATE ON, NOW?
Y-YOU THINK?
HEH!

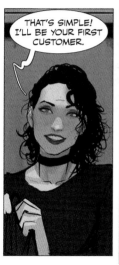

THAT'S SIMPLE! I'LL BE YOUR FIRST CUSTOMER.

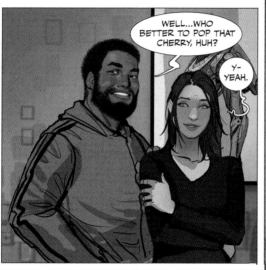

WELL...WHO BETTER TO POP THAT CHERRY, HUH?

Y-YEAH.

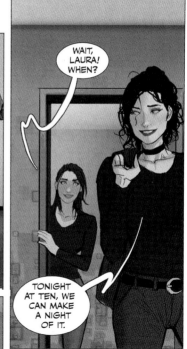

WAIT, LAURA! WHEN?

TONIGHT AT TEN, WE CAN MAKE A NIGHT OF IT.

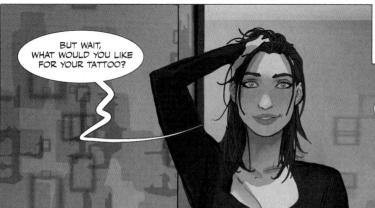

BUT WAIT, WHAT WOULD YOU LIKE FOR YOUR TATTOO?

I DON'T KNOW, SURPRISE ME!

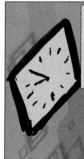

THE REST OF THE DAY I SPENT IN PANIC MODE, BECAUSE I HAD TO MAKE A PERMANENT PIECE OF ARTWORK USING NEEDLES ON THE SKIN OF THE WOMAN I LOVE.

Y'KNOW...NO PRESSURE.

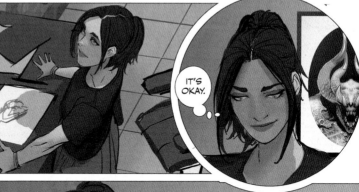

IT'S OKAY.

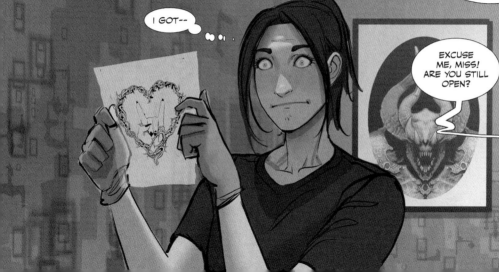

I GOT--

EXCUSE ME, MISS! ARE YOU STILL OPEN?

WELL?
Y-YEAH?
AAAAAA
GREAT! CAUSE IF YOU GOT THE INK, I GOT THE CANVAS!
COME ON.
LEMME KNOW IF IT HURTS TOO MUCH OR IS LIKE... TOO DEEP.
I ONLY EVER DID THIS ON, LIKE, ORANGES AND PIGSKIN...
NEITHER OF WHICH ARE BIG ON FEEDBACK.
YOU ALSO DID ONE ON THAT GUY IN HIGH SCHOOL.
OH GOD, DON'T REMIND ME.
IF THIS WORKS OUT FOR ME, I SHOULD PROBABLY HIT HIM UP AND FIX IT OR...I DUNNO, PAY FOR A LASER REMOVAL.

WELL, YOU'RE DOING GREAT SO FAR.
YEAH... FULL DISCLOSURE, I'M SINGING "POP GOES THE WEASEL" IN MY HEAD TO DISTRACT MYSELF AND STOP MY HANDS FROM SHAKING.
HAH! JACOB USED TO DO THAT.
WHO DO YOU THINK SUGGESTED IT?
BY THE WAY... I NEVER THANKED YOU FOR GETTING ME INTO THIS.
CLUMSY METHODS ASIDE.
HEY, IT WORKED!
THE WAY I SEE IT, IT'S A WIN/WIN...YOU GET TO LEARN THIS, AND I GET TO HAVE YOU BY MY SIDE MORE OFTEN. PLUS, I GET TO SAY THAT THE WOMAN I LOVE LEFT A PERMANENT MARK ON ME. THAT'S JUST COOL IN MY BOOK.

WELL?
BADASS!
OKAY...
SO YOU GOTTA KEEP THE FOIL ON...
MARIANNE...
...I'VE DONE THIS PART BEFORE.
STILL... IT NEVER MEANT THIS MUCH BEFORE.
YEAH... BRANDED BY THE ONE YOU LOVE.
KINDA KINKY, DON'T YOU THINK?

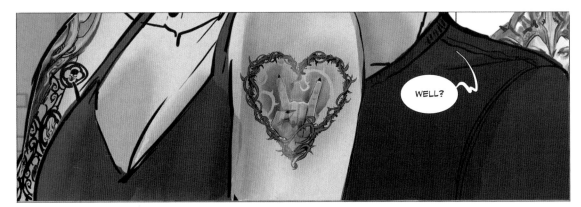

YEAH... KINDA.
WHAT ARE YOU DOING?
LAST TIME YOU PAID ME IN EXPOSURE...
...I HAPPEN TO LIKE THE CURRENCY.
I SEE...
WELL, I WAS ALWAYS KNOWN AS ONE WHO SETTLES HER DEBTS.

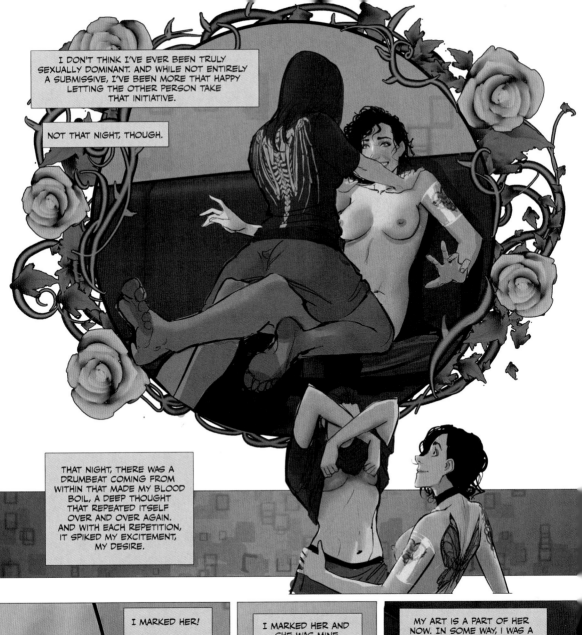

I DON'T THINK I'VE EVER BEEN TRULY SEXUALLY DOMINANT. AND WHILE NOT ENTIRELY A SUBMISSIVE, I'VE BEEN MORE THAT HAPPY LETTING THE OTHER PERSON TAKE THAT INITIATIVE.

NOT THAT NIGHT, THOUGH.

THAT NIGHT, THERE WAS A DRUMBEAT COMING FROM WITHIN THAT MADE MY BLOOD BOIL, A DEEP THOUGHT THAT REPEATED ITSELF OVER AND OVER AGAIN. AND WITH EACH REPETITION, IT SPIKED MY EXCITEMENT, MY DESIRE.

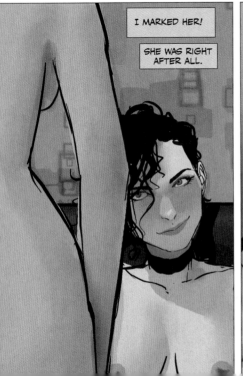

I MARKED HER!

SHE WAS RIGHT AFTER ALL.

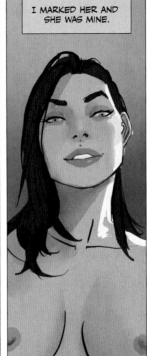

I MARKED HER AND SHE WAS MINE.

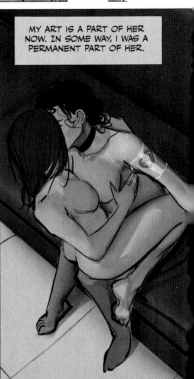

MY ART IS A PART OF HER NOW. IN SOME WAY, I WAS A PERMANENT PART OF HER.

IT WAS ALMOST LIKE I MARRIED HER THAT NIGHT... BOUND HER TO ME NOT WITH A RING OF GOLD, BUT WITH INK.
INK AND BLOOD...AND ON THAT WEDDING NIGHT OF OURS, I FELT A DEEP, UNRELENTING URGE TO TAKE IT FURTHER.
AFTER ALL, ONE DOES NOT WASTE A WEDDING NIGHT DOING NOTHING.
THE FIRST TIME, IT'S FAST, INTENSE...
...WE DROWN IN THIS AWKWARD, HYPER-PASSIONATE QUICKIE IN WHICH SHE FOUND A GREAT USE FOR MY THIGH...
...AND AN EVEN BETTER FUCKING USE FOR THROWING METAL HORNS. I GUESS YOU JUST CAN'T TAKE THE METAL OUT OF A METALHEAD!
BEFORE WE KNOW IT, IT'S OVER.
THE FIRST WAVE OF IT ALL CRASHES INTO US, LEAVING US WET AND GASPING FOR AIR, BUT I AM NOT SATISFIED. NOT DONE! NOT THAT NIGHT, NOT YET!
W-WOW.
THAT WAS--
A WARMUP.
NOW, DON'T GO ANYWHERE!

WHAT ARE YOU--
HEY! I SAID STAY RIGHT THERE!
I'M NOT DONE WITH YOU.
AND I WASN'T.
THE IDEA WAS STILL POUNDING IN MY HEAD AND LOWER PARTS LIKE A PRIMORDIAL, POSSESSIVE BEAT.
I MARKED HER!
I MARKED HER AND...
...SHE IS MINE!
WHAT ARE...
AND I WANTED TO MARK HER MORE.
...MMH!?

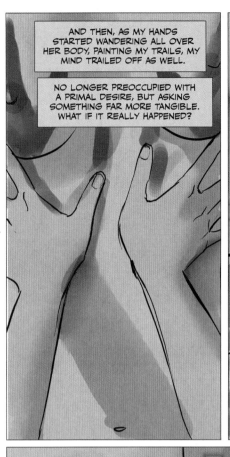

AND THEN, AS MY HANDS STARTED WANDERING ALL OVER HER BODY, PAINTING MY TRAILS, MY MIND TRAILED OFF AS WELL.

NO LONGER PREOCCUPIED WITH A PRIMAL DESIRE, BUT ASKING SOMETHING FAR MORE TANGIBLE. WHAT IF IT REALLY HAPPENED?

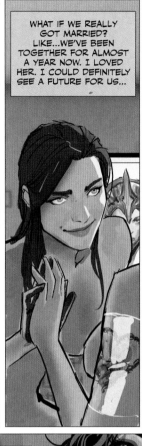

WHAT IF WE REALLY GOT MARRIED? LIKE...WE'VE BEEN TOGETHER FOR ALMOST A YEAR NOW. I LOVED HER. I COULD DEFINITELY SEE A FUTURE FOR US...

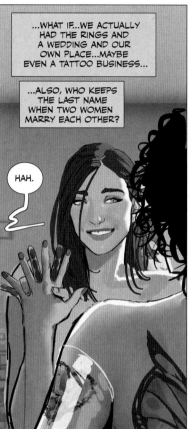

...WHAT IF...WE ACTUALLY HAD THE RINGS AND A WEDDING AND OUR OWN PLACE...MAYBE EVEN A TATTOO BUSINESS...

...ALSO, WHO KEEPS THE LAST NAME WHEN TWO WOMEN MARRY EACH OTHER?

HAH.

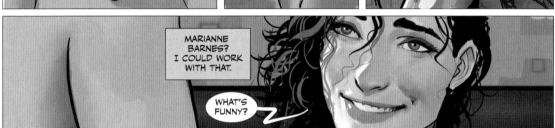

MARIANNE BARNES? I COULD WORK WITH THAT.

WHAT'S FUNNY?

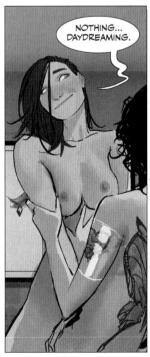

NOTHING... DAYDREAMING.

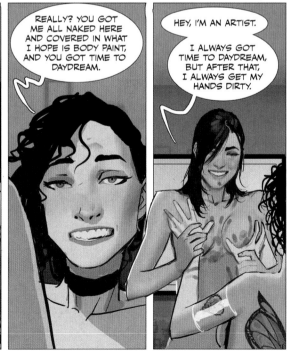

REALLY? YOU GOT ME ALL NAKED HERE AND COVERED IN WHAT I HOPE IS BODY PAINT, AND YOU GOT TIME TO DAYDREAM.

HEY, I'M AN ARTIST.

I ALWAYS GOT TIME TO DAYDREAM, BUT AFTER THAT, I ALWAYS GET MY HANDS DIRTY.

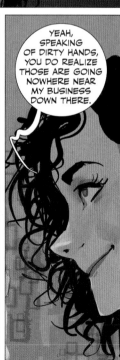

YEAH, SPEAKING OF DIRTY HANDS, YOU DO REALIZE THOSE ARE GOING NOWHERE NEAR MY BUSINESS DOWN THERE.

YOU UNDERESTIMATE ME.
TO QUOTE A KID ABOUT TO CRASH ON A BICYCLE--
HEY! DON'T YOU FUCKING SAY IT!
LOOK, MA! NO HANDS!
OH FUCK YO---OH ME!
DEFINITELY ME!

AS THE NIGHT WENT ON AND WE EVENTUALLY SANK INTO EACH OTHER'S ARMS, I THOUGHT THE ONLY TWO THOUGHTS MY MIND WOULD STILL ALLOW ME TO PROCESS...
...THE FIRST THOUGHT WAS THAT I LOVED HER DEEPLY.
MORE THAN ANYTHING...
...AND THE SECOND ONE: DON'T TOUCH THE FRESH TATTOO!

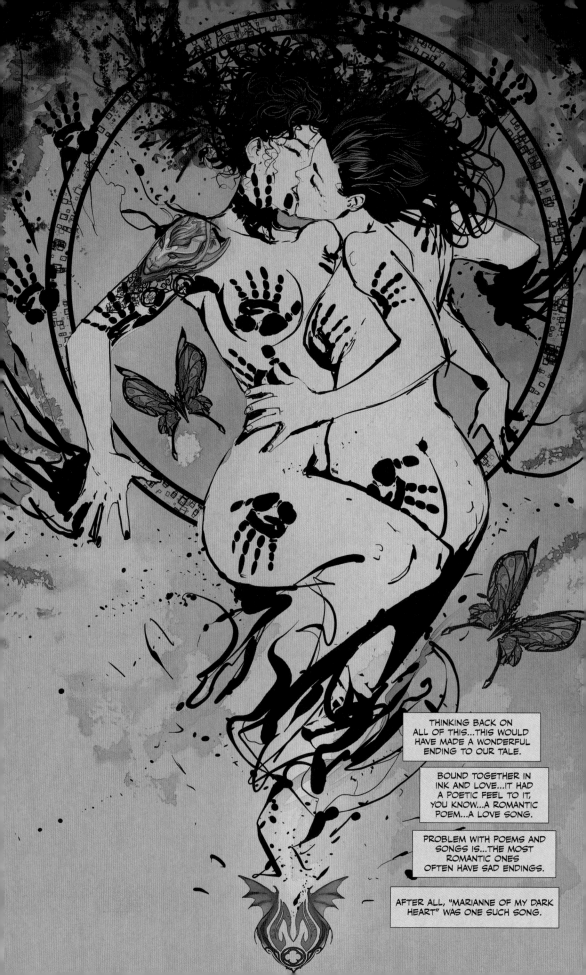

THINKING BACK ON ALL OF THIS...THIS WOULD HAVE MADE A WONDERFUL ENDING TO OUR TALE.

BOUND TOGETHER IN INK AND LOVE...IT HAD A POETIC FEEL TO IT, YOU KNOW...A ROMANTIC POEM...A LOVE SONG.

PROBLEM WITH POEMS AND SONGS IS...THE MOST ROMANTIC ONES OFTEN HAVE SAD ENDINGS.

AFTER ALL, "MARIANNE OF MY DARK HEART" WAS ONE SUCH SONG.

SHIT...HOW DO I FOLLOW AFTER THAT?, AH, WAIT! YES! AHEM! WHILE LAURA AND YOU SPENT YOUR TIME GETTING ALL HOT AND DIRTY ON YOUR WORKPLACE COUCH--
HEY, WE CLEANED AND DISINFECTED EVERYTHING INCLUDING THE BLOODY COUCH!
MHM, ANYWAYS, ALLY AND I HAD DEVOTED OURSELVES TO A PURER, INTELLECTUALLY ENLIGHTENED WAY OF LIFE.
MMM YES!
THAT WAS QUITE MARVELOUS.
UNBURDENED OF DECADENCY, WE SPENT MANY AN EARLY SUMMER AFTERNOON IN DISCUSSIONS OF AN INTELLECTUALLY STIMULATING NATURE...
WE REALLY SHOULD PARTAKE OF THIS CINEMATIC WONDER MORE OFTEN.
MMM, I MUST AGREE!
...WE SPENT MONTHS CONTEMPLATING DEEPER IMPLICATIONS OF MODERN WORKS OF ART...
...AND ...UH.
TO THINK ONE MIGHT FIND SUCH ENTERTAINMENT IN A SIMPLE TALE OF A PANDA LEARNING MARTIAL ARTS!
MOST UNEXPECTED!
INDEED, HAHAHAH!
SIGH...OKAY. WE WEREN'T QUITE *THAT* STIFF BUT, WE WERE IN THE NEIGHBORHOOD. THE REASON FOR IT WAS PRETTY OBVIOUS.
ALAN?
YEAH?
SO HOW LONG ARE WE GONNA KEEP IGNORING IT?

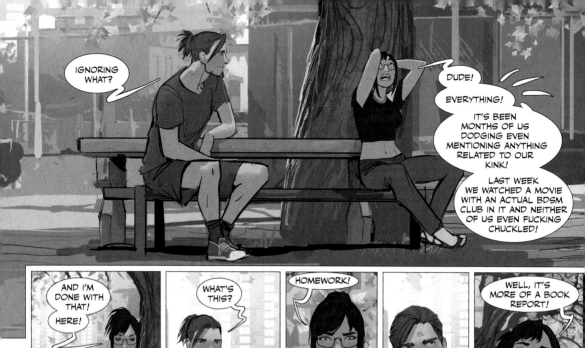

IGNORING WHAT?

DUDE!

EVERYTHING!

IT'S BEEN MONTHS OF US DODGING EVEN MENTIONING ANYTHING RELATED TO OUR KINK!

LAST WEEK WE WATCHED A MOVIE WITH AN ACTUAL BDSM CLUB IN IT AND NEITHER OF US EVEN FUCKING CHUCKLED!

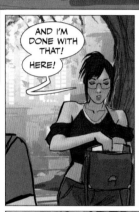

AND I'M DONE WITH THAT!

HERE!

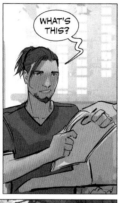

WHAT'S THIS?

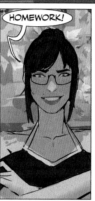

HOMEWORK!

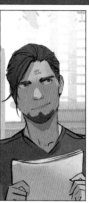

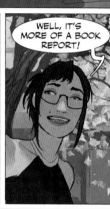

WELL, IT'S MORE OF A BOOK REPORT!

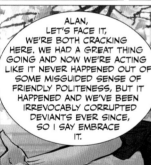

ALAN, LET'S FACE IT, WE'RE BOTH CRACKING HERE. WE HAD A GREAT THING GOING AND NOW WE'RE ACTING LIKE IT NEVER HAPPENED OUT OF SOME MISGUIDED SENSE OF FRIENDLY POLITENESS, BUT IT HAPPENED AND WE'VE BEEN IRREVOCABLY CORRUPTED DEVIANTS EVER SINCE, SO I SAY EMBRACE IT.

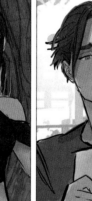

THE FUCK DID YOU PRINT OUT? A PERVERTED MANIFESTO? I MEAN, I'M IN BY DEFAULT.

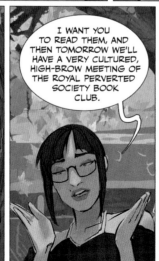

HEH! NOT QUITE! YOU REMEMBER WHEN I SAID MY BIG MASTURBATION FUEL IS ONLINE STORIES?

WELL I MADE A SELECTION OF SOME GOOD ONES.

I WANT YOU TO READ THEM, AND THEN TOMORROW WE'LL HAVE A VERY CULTURED, HIGH-BROW MEETING OF THE ROYAL PERVERTED SOCIETY BOOK CLUB.

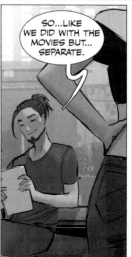

SO...LIKE WE DID WITH THE MOVIES BUT... SEPARATE.

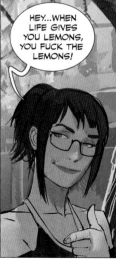

HEY...WHEN LIFE GIVES YOU LEMONS, YOU FUCK THE LEMONS!

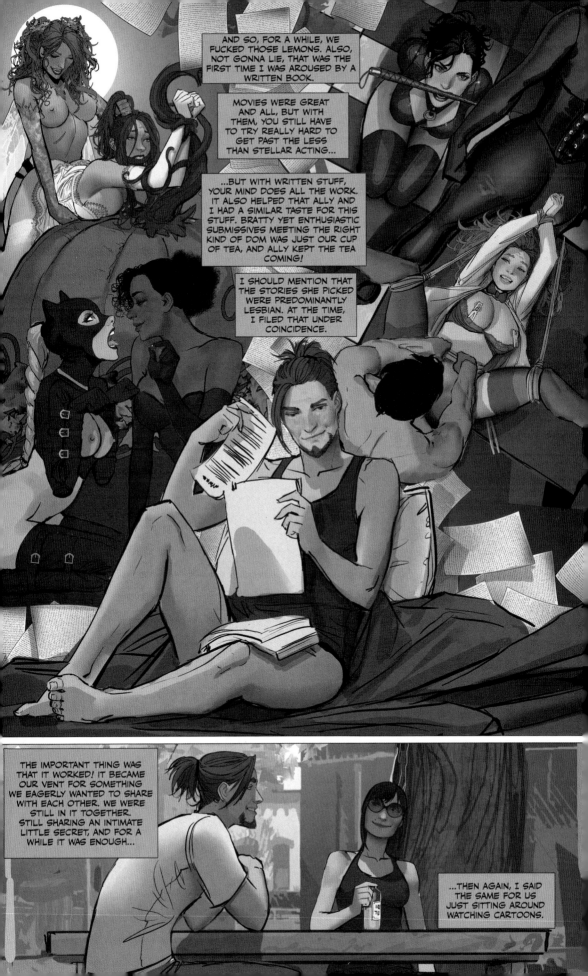

AND SO, FOR A WHILE, WE FUCKED THOSE LEMONS. ALSO, NOT GONNA LIE, THAT WAS THE FIRST TIME I WAS AROUSED BY A WRITTEN BOOK.

MOVIES WERE GREAT AND ALL, BUT WITH THEM, YOU STILL HAVE TO TRY REALLY HARD TO GET PAST THE LESS THAN STELLAR ACTING...

...BUT WITH WRITTEN STUFF, YOUR MIND DOES ALL THE WORK. IT ALSO HELPED THAT ALLY AND I HAD A SIMILAR TASTE FOR THIS STUFF. BRATTY YET ENTHUSIASTIC SUBMISSIVES MEETING THE RIGHT KIND OF DOM WAS JUST OUR CUP OF TEA, AND ALLY KEPT THE TEA COMING!

I SHOULD MENTION THAT THE STORIES SHE PICKED WERE PREDOMINANTLY LESBIAN. AT THE TIME, I FILED THAT UNDER COINCIDENCE.

THE IMPORTANT THING WAS THAT IT WORKED! IT BECAME OUR VENT FOR SOMETHING WE EAGERLY WANTED TO SHARE WITH EACH OTHER. WE WERE STILL IN IT TOGETHER. STILL SHARING AN INTIMATE LITTLE SECRET, AND FOR A WHILE IT WAS ENOUGH...

...THEN AGAIN, I SAID THE SAME FOR US JUST SITTING AROUND WATCHING CARTOONS.

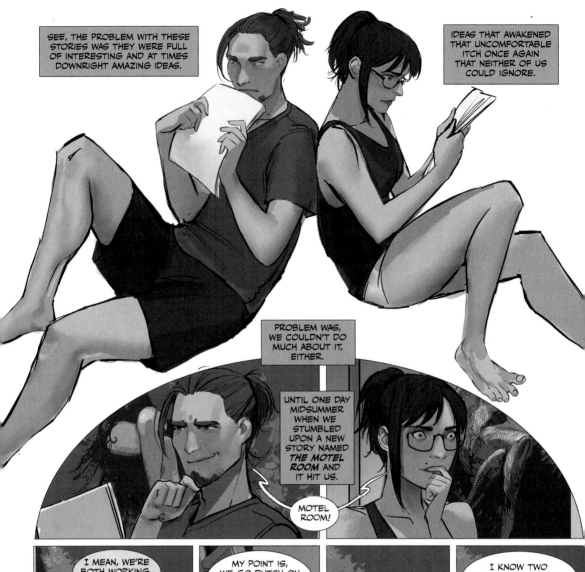

SEE, THE PROBLEM WITH THESE STORIES WAS THEY WERE FULL OF INTERESTING AND AT TIMES DOWNRIGHT AMAZING IDEAS.

IDEAS THAT AWAKENED THAT UNCOMFORTABLE ITCH ONCE AGAIN THAT NEITHER OF US COULD IGNORE.

PROBLEM WAS, WE COULDN'T DO MUCH ABOUT IT, EITHER.

UNTIL ONE DAY MIDSUMMER WHEN WE STUMBLED UPON A NEW STORY NAMED *THE MOTEL ROOM* AND IT HIT US.

MOTEL ROOM!

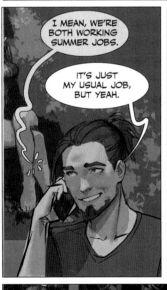

I MEAN, WE'RE BOTH WORKING SUMMER JOBS.

IT'S JUST MY USUAL JOB, BUT YEAH.

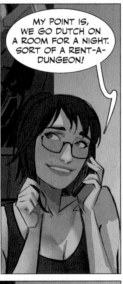

MY POINT IS, WE GO DUTCH ON A ROOM FOR A NIGHT. SORT OF A RENT-A-DUNGEON!

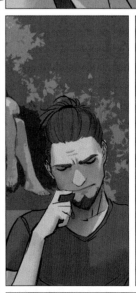

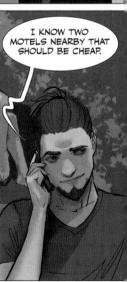

I KNOW TWO MOTELS NEARBY THAT SHOULD BE CHEAP.

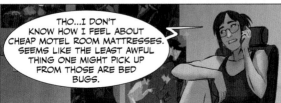

THO...I DON'T KNOW HOW I FEEL ABOUT CHEAP MOTEL ROOM MATTRESSES. SEEMS LIKE THE LEAST AWFUL THING ONE MIGHT PICK UP FROM THOSE ARE BED BUGS.

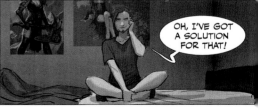

OH, I'VE GOT A SOLUTION FOR THAT!

WE MET THAT WEEKEND AT THE MOTEL. I WAS THERE EARLIER TO PREPARE THE ROOM AND...WELL...YOU KNOW HOW SOMETIMES YOU GET THIS IDEA, BUT ONCE YOU ACTUALLY GET IT DONE IT'S NOTHING LIKE YOU ENVISIONED IT?
WELL...
HEY, WHY THE LONG FACE?
DID YOU LOCK YOURSELF OUT?
WHAT? NO!
AND...
...YOU LOOK GREAT.
AWW, THANK YOU. SO? COME ON! WE GOING IN OR WHAT?!
AH...IN. RIGHT!
ABOUT THAT--
WHAT? YOU GOT THE ROOM?
OH I GOT IT... AND I PREPPED IT, IT'S JUST...
...WELL...UH, I GUESS I MAY AS WELL SHOW YOU.

SEE, I WANTED TO SOLVE THE PROBLEM WITH THE QUESTIONABLE MATTRESS HYGIENE. THE MOTEL DOES HAVE RUBBER SHEETS FOR GUESTS WITH TODDLERS, BUT THOSE WERE SUSPICIOUSLY YELLOW SO I DECIDED TO IMPROVISE. I BOUGHT SOME PROTECTIVE PLASTIC, SOME DUCT TAPE.
POINT IS, ALL OF THIS LOOKED *WAAAY* BETTER IN MY HEAD.
JESUS, DEXTER!
OH, FUCK OFF!
BUT ALSO, YEAH. THE PLACE NOW LOOKS LIKE A FUCKING KILL ROOM!
SORRY.
HMM...
...I CAN WORK WITH THIS!
WHAT? ALSO, SHOULD I BE WORRIED?
NO. IN FACT... THIS IS PROBABLY THE BEST THING YOU COULD HAVE DONE. REMEMBER THE BABY OIL?
LAST TIME WE ONLY USED A LITTLE. TODAY, WE'RE USING A LOT!
OOOH!
NOW, GET NAKED, GREASE UP!

BECAUSE I'M ABOUT TO WRESTLE YOU FOR WHO GETS TO DOMINATE TONIGHT!
A PROGRAMMER VERSUS SOMEONE WHO WORKS WITH HIS HANDS EVERY DAY?
I LIKE MY ODDS!

OH BUT I FORGOT TO MENTION. YOU CUM, YOU LOSE BY DEFAULT!
OH FUCK OFF! YOU'LL CHEAT!
SQUIRT
OF COURSE!
NOW, INTO THE RING!
ALLEY--
--OOP---
---W---
SHLPPPP
ALLY!!!
WAH!
SCHLICC
THUD
ALLY? YOU OKAY?
OW, YEAH!
DOES THAT COUNT AS A RING OUT? DID YOU JUST LOSE?
I DON'T KNOW, LET'S ASK THE JUDGES!

YEAH...THE MOTEL THING DIDN'T REALLY WORK OUT. NOT JUST BECAUSE OF THE SLIP AND SLIDE MISHAP, MIND YOU!
SEE, FIRST THERE WERE THE RANDOM PEOPLE STANDING OUTSIDE DRINKING AND TALKING LOUDLY.
ARGH! DUDE, FOCUS!
IT'S NOT THAT EASY, OKAY?
SO JENKINS CALLS IN BECAUSE THE PRINTER IS CHEWING UP THE PAPERS, RIGHT?
YEAH?
AND THEN LATER IN THE EVENING, AN ARGUMENT BROKE OUT IN THE ROOM NEXT TO US.
THEN EXPLAIN TO ME WHY THERE WAS A JIZZ-FILLED CONDOM IN THE BACK SEAT OF OUR CAR!?
YOU KNOW WHAT...THE MOOD IS KINDA GONE.
YEAH.
AND THAT WENT ON, AND ON, AND ON...
YOU DREW LITTLE HEARTS ON HIS CARD!!!
SHIT! HE GOT HER THERE!
MHM...
BABY, LET'S TALK ABOUT THIS!
OH FOR FUCK'S SAKE! YOU TALKED ENOUGH! QUIT BEING SUCH A FUCKING DOORMAT AND DUMP HER CHEATING ASS!
I HOPE YOU HAD A PLEASANT STAY.
HRMPF.
IN THE END, WE ADMITTED OUR DEFEAT AND MADE PEACE WITH THE FACT THAT, BAR SOME MIRACLE, OUR EXPERIMENTING DAYS WERE OVER.

AND THEN, ONE DAY AT THE VERY END OF THE SUMMER, WE GOT OUR MIRACLE.
'SCUSE ME, COMIN' THROUGH.
CHRIS? WHAT ARE YOU DOING HERE?
OH, HEY ALAN, NOTHING MUCH, PAYING MY BILLS.
THEY'RE REMODELLING THREE CLASSROOMS AND THEY ARE PAYING A FEW OF US TO GET THE OLD FURNITURE OUT.
SO, IS YOUR DAD'S COMPANY MAKING THE NEW FURNITURE, OR?
NAH, I'M JUST HERE FREELANCE HAULING STUFF.
IS THERE A LOT OF IT?
KINDA.
WE'RE LOADING THE SECOND TRUCK NOW.
DAMN, SOME OF THIS STUFF IS QUALITY WOOD. WELL MADE. HELL, I'VE DONE RESTORATIONS ON FAR CHEAPER STUFF.
SO, WHAT, THEY'RE JUST THROWING ALL THESE AWAY?
HONESTLY?
NO IDEA. YOU SHOULD PROBABLY ASK THE JANITOR.

YUP, THROWING IT ALL AWAY. WE USED TO STORE OLD STUFF LIKE THIS UP IN THE ATTIC SPACE, BUT THE DAMN THING IS PROBABLY FULL OF OLD GYM EQUIPMENT AND DESKS BY NOW.
PROBABLY FULL?
YEAH. WE LOST THE ATTIC KEY A FEW YEARS AGO.
I MEAN, IT'S NOT A BIG DEAL TO CHANGE A LOCK.
YOU'D THINK SO. BUT YOU THROW BUREAUCRACY INTO THE MIX, AND EVEN MAKING A BLOODY BOWL OF CEREAL BECOMES A TWELVE-HOUR JOB.
I ASKED THE COLLEGE TO PAY FOR A LOCKSMITH, BUT THEY SAID, "YOU'RE THE JANITOR, CAN'T YOU DO IT?" SO I TOLD THEM NEXT TIME A HISTORY PROFESSOR IS SICK, JUST SEND IN THE MATH GUY. SEE HOW WELL THAT GOES.
SO INSTEAD OF PAYING THE LOCKSMITH, THEY'RE PAYING TO HAVE ALL OF THIS JUNKED.
SOMETHING LIKE THAT.
AH WELL... ROCK AND A HARD PLACE, I GUESS. SEE YA, CHRIS.
SEE YA, DUDE!
IT'S FUNNY, REALLY. AS SOMEONE IN THE BUSINESS OF RESTORING STUFF, MY INTEREST REALLY WAS PURELY PROFESSIONAL...
HEH... DAMN...A WHOLE ATTIC FULL OF GYM EQUIPMENT AND OLD FURNITURE.
...AT FIRST.

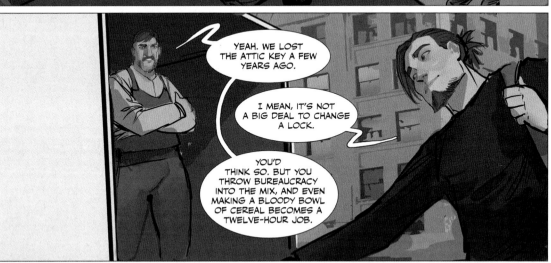

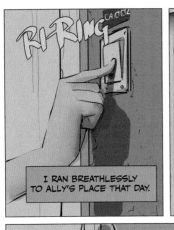

RI-RING

I RAN BREATHLESSLY TO ALLY'S PLACE THAT DAY.

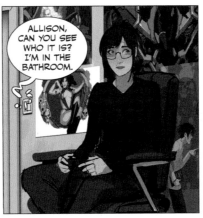

ALLISON, CAN YOU SEE WHO IT IS? I'M IN THE BATHROOM.

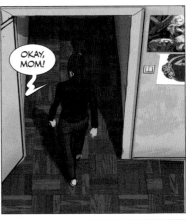

OKAY, MOM!

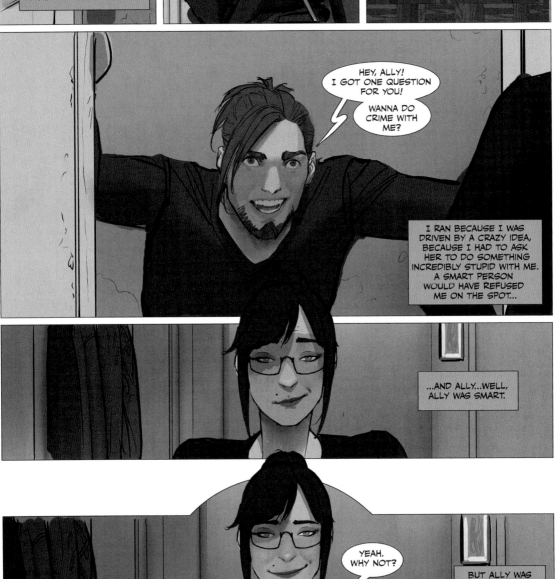

HEY, ALLY! I GOT ONE QUESTION FOR YOU!

WANNA DO CRIME WITH ME?

I RAN BECAUSE I WAS DRIVEN BY A CRAZY IDEA, BECAUSE I HAD TO ASK HER TO DO SOMETHING INCREDIBLY STUPID WITH ME. A SMART PERSON WOULD HAVE REFUSED ME ON THE SPOT...

...AND ALLY...WELL, ALLY WAS SMART.

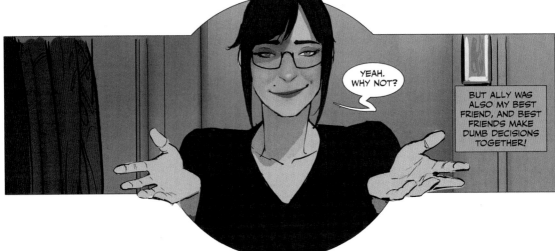

YEAH. WHY NOT?

BUT ALLY WAS ALSO MY BEST FRIEND, AND BEST FRIENDS MAKE DUMB DECISIONS TOGETHER!

MEANWHILE, MY DUMB DECISION WAS MINE ALONE.
IT WAS MY TWENTIETH BIRTHDAY, AND I WAS A RESPONSIBLE GIRL WITH LONG-TERM PLANS.
THE WAY I SAW IT, I HAD THE RIGHT TO ONE DUMB DECISION AND I PICKED MINE.
COME ON, IT'S GONNA LOOK GREAT!
ON YOUR BACK?
YEAH.
A BAND LOGO?
YEAH!
OKAY ANNE, REMEMBER MY LITTLE TALK ABOUT DISSUADING YOUR CUSTOMERS FROM THE BIG TATTOO MISTAKES IN LIFE?
THE BAND LOGOS...
...THEIR LOVERS' NAMES.
AND ANYTHING SNOOPY-RELATED, I KNOW!
BUT THIS BAND IS HOW I MET LAURA AND IT ALWAYS MAKES ME SMILE--
SO TECHNICALLY, THIS BAND LOGO IS YOUR LOVER'S NAME AT THE SAME TIME...WANT ME TO ADD WOODSTOCK PERCHED ON TOP OF IT SO THAT YOU'RE KINDA THREE FOR THREE?

HEH! FUCK YOU! WHAT'S IT GONNA COST ME?
NOTHING. IT'S MY NON-RETURNABLE BIRTHDAY GIFT TO YOU!
NON-RETURNABLE BEING THE OPERATIVE WORD HERE.
JACOB, YOU ARE THE BEST!!
UHUH, JUST DON'T GO TOO WILD TONIGHT. I GOT YOU A CUSTOMER TOMORROW!
OF COURSE NOT! I JUST TURNED TWENTY, I'M NOT ALLOWED TO DRINK!
HAH!
HEY, SEXY!
GOING MY WAY?
WHA-- WHAT HAPPENNED TO THE HARLEY?
YEAH...UH, SO I HAD THIS IDEA OF SURPRISING YOU BY PICKING YOU UP ON IT TODAY BUT TURNS OUT THAT SPECIFIC MODEL IS NOT REALLY TWO-PERSON FRIENDLY.
THANK GOD I CHECKED WITH A BUDDY OF MINE. THEN AGAIN, MY UNCLE DID GET THAT BIKE FOR HIS MIDLIFE CRISIS SO...GUESS IT MAKES SENSE IT'S A SOLO BIKE.
ANYHOW, LONG STORY SHORT, I BORROWED THIS BAD BOY FROM A FRIEND!

WHY DO I GET THE PINK HELMET?
NOW HOP ON, BIRTHDAY GIRL, I'M TAKING YOU SOMEWHERE AWESOME!
BECAUSE IT SUITS YOU, BLONDIE!
OH... THE JIG IS UP, THEN?
HOW DID YOU NOTICE?
FOUND SOME POORLY DYED HAIRS ON MY BED THE LAST TIME YOU WERE THERE.
WELL THERE GOES MY COOL DARK FACADE--
YOU DO KNOW MY HAIR COLOR IS ACTUALLY BROWN, RIGHT?!
OMG! YOU FUCKING PHONY!!!
HAHAHAHAH!
IT WAS MY TWENTIETH BIRTHDAY...
AN IMPORTANT DAY NOT BECAUSE OF ME, BUT BECAUSE OF US.

SEE, ON THAT DAY, AS I RODE BEHIND MY GIRLFRIEND ON A BORROWED VESPA, I THOUGHT IT ALL SOMEHOW FELT...REAL.
NOT A FANTASY OF SOME BADASS DARK CHICK AND ME ON A HARLEY BEING ALL DANGEROUS BUT JUST... LAURA AND ME. ON A VESPA, A BLONDE AND A BRUNETTE WEARING OUR EDGINESS ON THE SURFACE WHILE BEING ALL MUSHY IN THE MIDDLE.
THERE WAS THAT FEELING THAT WE GOT TO THAT STAGE OF THINGS WHERE WE DROPPED OUR PRETENSE AND COULD JUST BE OURSELVES.
HEY, WHEN I SAID HOLD ON, I DIDN'T MEAN TO MY TITS!
YES YOU DID!
I FELT SO PROFOUNDLY HAPPY THAT DAY. LITTLE DID I KNOW, IT WOULD ONLY GET BETTER, BECAUSE LAURA HAD A SURPRISE PLANNED OUT FOR ME, AND THIS ONE WOULD BE AMAZING. YOU KNOW...FOR A CHANGE.

HERE'S TO US!
TO US.
AND HERE'S TO NEXT YEAR WHEN I CAN LEGALLY BUY YOU A BEER!
NICE TO KNOW WE HAVE A FUTURE.
I MEAN...YEAH? WAS THERE EVEN A QUESTION?
HEH!
BUT LISTEN, I'VE BEEN THINKING.
WHAT?
HEY, GIRLS, SORRY, WE'RE HAVING AN EARLY LAST CALL! WE NEED TO CHECK IF YOU HAVE THE TOKENS, 'CAUSE THE BAR IS BOOKED FROM 8 FOR THE REST OF THE NIGHT AND ONLY PEOPLE WITH TOKENS CAN STAY.
TOKENS?

ALL GOOD.

JESUS, I NEARLY HAD A HEART ATTACK THERE. I THOUGHT HE HEARD ME SAYING I WAS TWENTY. AHHAHA!

BUT--WAIT, WHAT ARE THOSE TOKENS? WHAT'S GOING--

HEY, EVERYBODY. YOU'LL NEVER GUESS WHO I FOUND LOITERING IN FRONT OF THE BAR!

MUH--M--

THEY ARE HAVING A PARTY CELEBRATING THEIR ALBUM RELEASE FOR FRIENDS AND SELECT FANS!

AND WE'VE BEEN SELECTED?

HELL NO, I HAD TO WORK MY ASS OFF TO GET THESE TOKENS. BUT SEEING YOU LIKE THIS...

...FUCKING WORTH IT! HAPPY BIRTHDAY, MARIANNE!

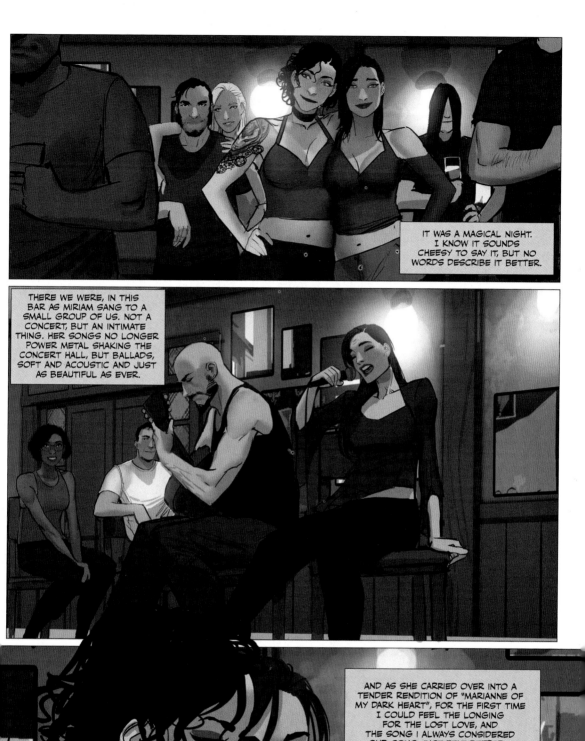

IT WAS A MAGICAL NIGHT. I KNOW IT SOUNDS CHEESY TO SAY IT, BUT NO WORDS DESCRIBE IT BETTER.

THERE WE WERE, IN THIS BAR AS MIRIAM SANG TO A SMALL GROUP OF US. NOT A CONCERT, BUT AN INTIMATE THING. HER SONGS NO LONGER POWER METAL SHAKING THE CONCERT HALL, BUT BALLADS, SOFT AND ACOUSTIC AND JUST AS BEAUTIFUL AS EVER.

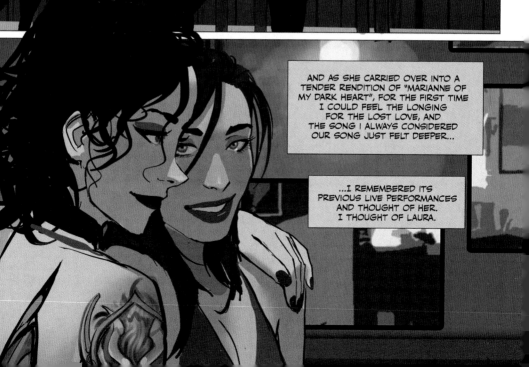

AND AS SHE CARRIED OVER INTO A TENDER RENDITION OF "MARIANNE OF MY DARK HEART", FOR THE FIRST TIME I COULD FEEL THE LONGING FOR THE LOST LOVE, AND THE SONG I ALWAYS CONSIDERED OUR SONG JUST FELT DEEPER...

...I REMEMBERED ITS PREVIOUS LIVE PERFORMANCES AND THOUGHT OF HER. I THOUGHT OF LAURA.

I THOUGHT OF THE NIGHT WE SANG IT TOGETHER FOR THE FIRST TIME.
AND EVERY FOLLOWING TIME.
YES, IT WAS A LOVELY SONG.
IT WAS OUR SONG....
...THEN AND THERE IN LAURA'S ARMS, I THOUGHT, THIS NIGHT COULDN'T GET ANY BETTER.

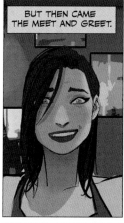

BUT THEN CAME THE MEET AND GREET.

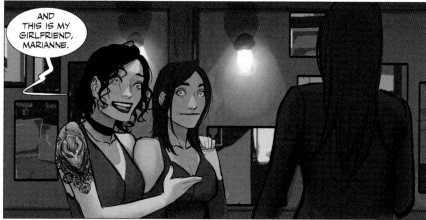

AND THIS IS MY GIRLFRIEND, MARIANNE.

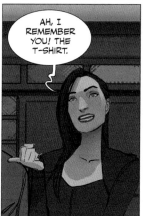

AH, I REMEMBER YOU! THE T-SHIRT.

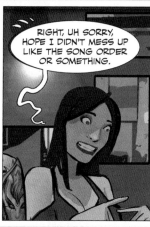

RIGHT, UH SORRY, HOPE I DIDN'T MESS UP LIKE THE SONG ORDER OR SOMETHING.

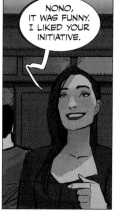

NONO, IT WAS FUNNY. I LIKED YOUR INITIATIVE.

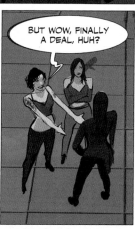

BUT WOW, FINALLY A DEAL, HUH?

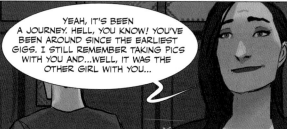

YEAH, IT'S BEEN A JOURNEY. HELL, YOU KNOW! YOU'VE BEEN AROUND SINCE THE EARLIEST GIGS. I STILL REMEMBER TAKING PICS WITH YOU AND...WELL, IT WAS THE OTHER GIRL WITH YOU...

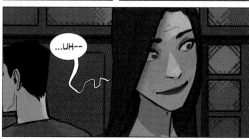

...UH--

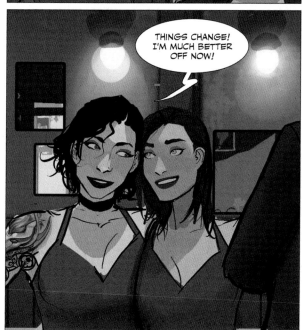

THINGS CHANGE! I'M MUCH BETTER OFF NOW!

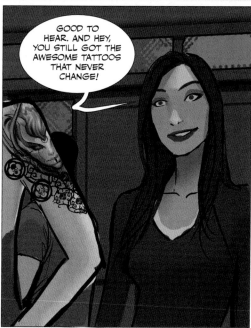

GOOD TO HEAR. AND HEY, YOU STILL GOT THE AWESOME TATTOOS THAT NEVER CHANGE!

WELL, ACTUALLY, I GOT A NEW ONE, COURTESY OF MARIANNE HERE.
HOLY CRAP, THAT'S COOL. YOU DO TATTOOS?
UH YEAH?
COULD YOU DO ONE FOR ME? I'LL PAY, OF COURSE.
I, UH... OF C-COURSE!
OKAY, LAURA, I'LL STEAL YOUR GIRLFRIEND AWAY FROM YOU FOR A FEW MINUTES. I WANNA GET HER TO MEET THE OTHERS, AND ALSO I'VE GOT A NOTEBOOK SO WE CAN JOT DOWN THE DETAILS.
THAT OKAY WITH YOU?
UH...SURE.
GREAT! WON'T BE TOO LONG.
IT WAS ALL SO SURREAL! THERE I WAS, ABOUT TO TALK TO MY FAVORITE SINGER ABOUT WHAT KIND OF A TATTOO SHE WANTED, AND EVEN IN THAT CRAZY MOMENT, I COULDN'T STOP THINKING OF LAURA.
IT WAS ALL BECAUSE OF HER. THIS WONDERFUL WOMAN WHO COULD HAVE THEN AND THERE ASKED ME TO MARRY HER AND I WOULD HAVE SAID YES. THAT'S HOW MUCH I LOVED HER.

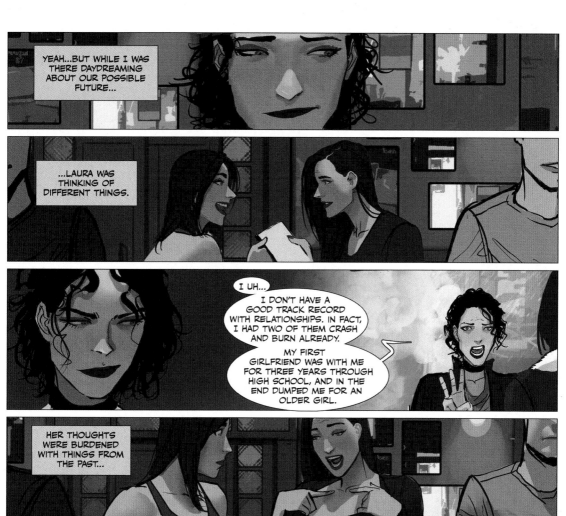

YEAH...BUT WHILE I WAS THERE DAYDREAMING ABOUT OUR POSSIBLE FUTURE...

...LAURA WAS THINKING OF DIFFERENT THINGS.

I UH...

I DON'T HAVE A GOOD TRACK RECORD WITH RELATIONSHIPS. IN FACT, I HAD TWO OF THEM CRASH AND BURN ALREADY.

MY FIRST GIRLFRIEND WAS WITH ME FOR THREE YEARS THROUGH HIGH SCHOOL, AND IN THE END DUMPED ME FOR AN OLDER GIRL.

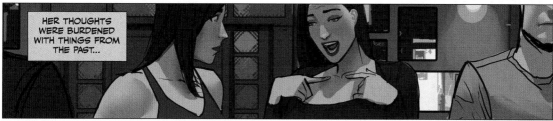

HER THOUGHTS WERE BURDENED WITH THINGS FROM THE PAST...

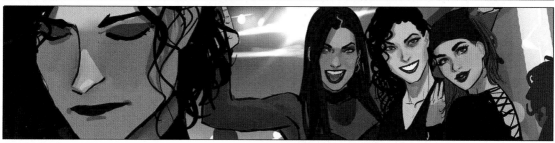

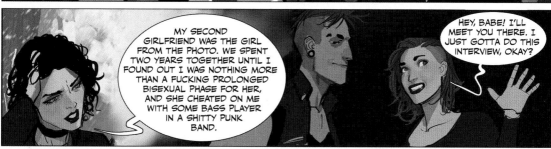

MY SECOND GIRLFRIEND WAS THE GIRL FROM THE PHOTO. WE SPENT TWO YEARS TOGETHER UNTIL I FOUND OUT I WAS NOTHING MORE THAN A FUCKING PROLONGED BISEXUAL PHASE FOR HER, AND SHE CHEATED ON ME WITH SOME BASS PLAYER IN A SHITTY PUNK BAND.

HEY, BABE! I'LL MEET YOU THERE. I JUST GOTTA DO THIS INTERVIEW, OKAY?

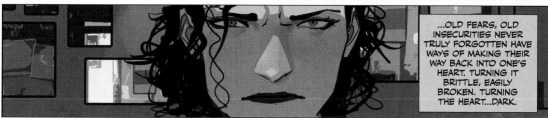

...OLD FEARS, OLD INSECURITIES NEVER TRULY FORGOTTEN HAVE WAYS OF MAKING THEIR WAY BACK INTO ONE'S HEART. TURNING IT BRITTLE, EASILY BROKEN. TURNING THE HEART...DARK.

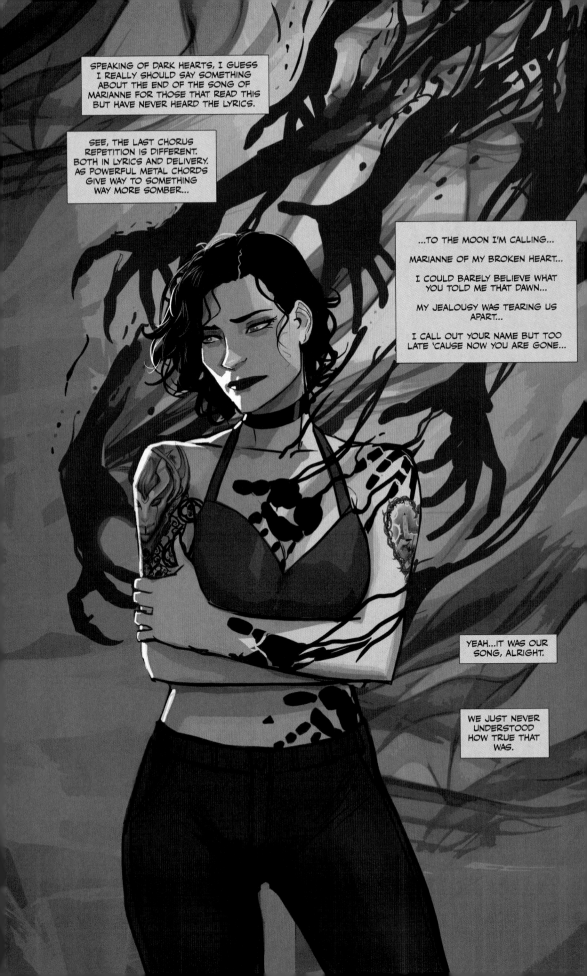

SPEAKING OF DARK HEARTS, I GUESS I REALLY SHOULD SAY SOMETHING ABOUT THE END OF THE SONG OF MARIANNE FOR THOSE THAT READ THIS BUT HAVE NEVER HEARD THE LYRICS.

SEE, THE LAST CHORUS REPETITION IS DIFFERENT. BOTH IN LYRICS AND DELIVERY. AS POWERFUL METAL CHORDS GIVE WAY TO SOMETHING WAY MORE SOMBER...

...TO THE MOON I'M CALLING...

MARIANNE OF MY BROKEN HEART...

I COULD BARELY BELIEVE WHAT YOU TOLD ME THAT DAWN...

MY JEALOUSY WAS TEARING US APART...

I CALL OUT YOUR NAME BUT TOO LATE 'CAUSE NOW YOU ARE GONE...

YEAH...IT WAS OUR SONG, ALRIGHT.

WE JUST NEVER UNDERSTOOD HOW TRUE THAT WAS.

I KNOW I HEARD SOMEONE UP HERE! I SWEAR IF I CATCH ANY OF YOU SMOKING IN THIS HALLWAY, THERE'LL BE HELL TO PAY!
NEXT VOLUME! THINGS GET DUMB WITH PERVERTS IN THE ATTIC!

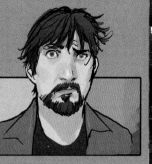

HERE WE ARE AGAIN

ANOTHER YEAR, ANOTHER SUNSTONE. ONLY THIRTEEN MORE TO GO. THIS ONE IS WHAT I CALL MY CALM BEFORE THE STORM. IT IS THE GOOD TIMES, THE TIMES WHEN THINGS JUST SEEMED TO WORK FOR OUR PROTAGONISTS.

THERE IS A JOY TO WRITING A RELATIONSHIP JUST CHUGGING ALONG. PEELING OFF THE VENEER AND THE HIGH POLISH OF PRETENSE, AND FINDING THE REAL PERSON IN FRONT OF YOU. IN A WAY, THIS IS THE REAL TEST OF ANY RELATIONSHIP. MEETING YOUR SIGNIFICANT OTHER, NOT AT THEIR VERY BEST, BUT AT THEIR EVERY DAY, AND YES, AT TIMES AT THEIR VERY WORST.

IT IS THAT VERY WORST THAT WILL, IN THE END, DESTROY A RELATIONSHIP THAT HAD EVERYTHING GOING FOR IT.

THIS BRINGS ME TO LAURA. PROBABLY MY ABSOLUTE FAVORITE CHARACTER TO WRITE IN THIS STORY ARC. AN INSECURE, BIPHOBIC MESS OF A METALHEAD THAT MEANS THE VERY BEST, BUT EVERY TIME FINDS A WAY TO PUT HER FOOT IN IT.

UNFORTUNATELY, IN THE NEXT VOLUME, HER WORST QUALITIES ARE ABOUT TO DESTROY SOMETHING BEAUTIFUL. STILL, DON'T YOU WRITE HER OFF QUITE YET. SHE DOES COME BACK LATER IN THE ARC. LIKE GANDALF WHEN HE WAS MOST NEEDED, LAURA THE WHITE WILL COME TO ANNE'S AID, AS BETWEEN THE VOLUMES, SHE DID THIS UNEXPECTED THING...

...SHE GOT HELP.

MORE ON THAT AND OF LAURA'S STRANGE NEW RELATIONSHIP IN DUE TIME. FOR NOW, I LEAVE YOU WITH SOME BONUS STUFF. IT WAS A STRANGE YEAR FOR EVERYONE AND I FOUND SOME SOLACE IN HUMOR AS I OFTEN DO.

ANYHOW. BACK TO WORK, THESE VOLUMES WON'T MAKE THEMSELVES.

SEE YOU NEXT YEAR, BUT TILL THEN, MAYBE TAKE A LOOK AT MY OTHER WORKS. THERE IS A CERTAIN BOOK CALLED *FINE PRINT* THAT MIGHT BE OF SOME INTEREST TO SUNSTONE FANS.

HEY, LORD VADER! YOU DONE IN THERE OR WHAT?

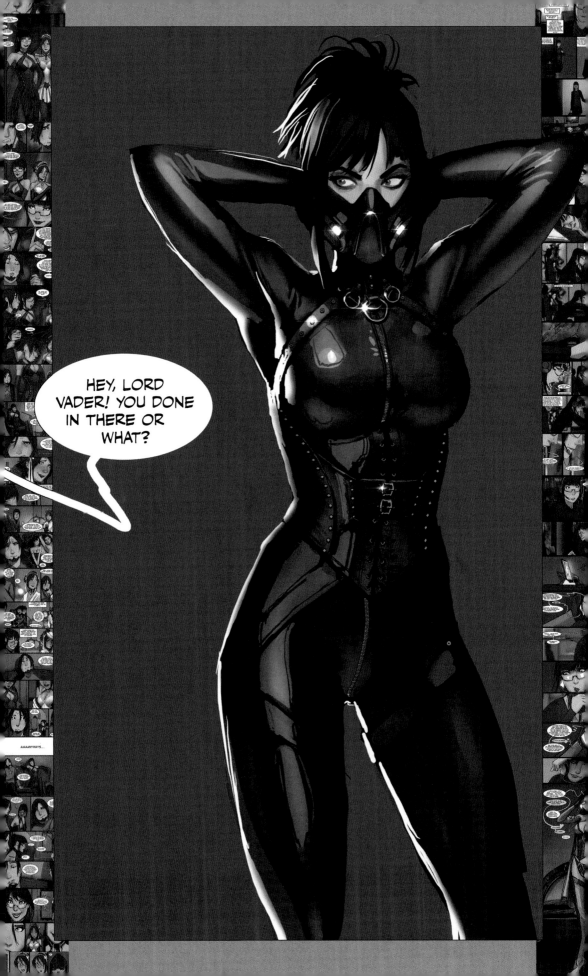

OKAY, KITTEN! YOU WILL COUNT EACH AND EVERY BEAD I PULL OUT, AND THANK ME FOR EVERY ONE OF THEM AS YOU DO!
ARE WE CLEAR?
BUT MISTRESS! I'M A CAT! CAT'S CAN'T COUNT!
THOSE FUCKING BRATTY SUBS!

COME OOON!

BUT...
THE NEW RAID!
GOOD GIRL!

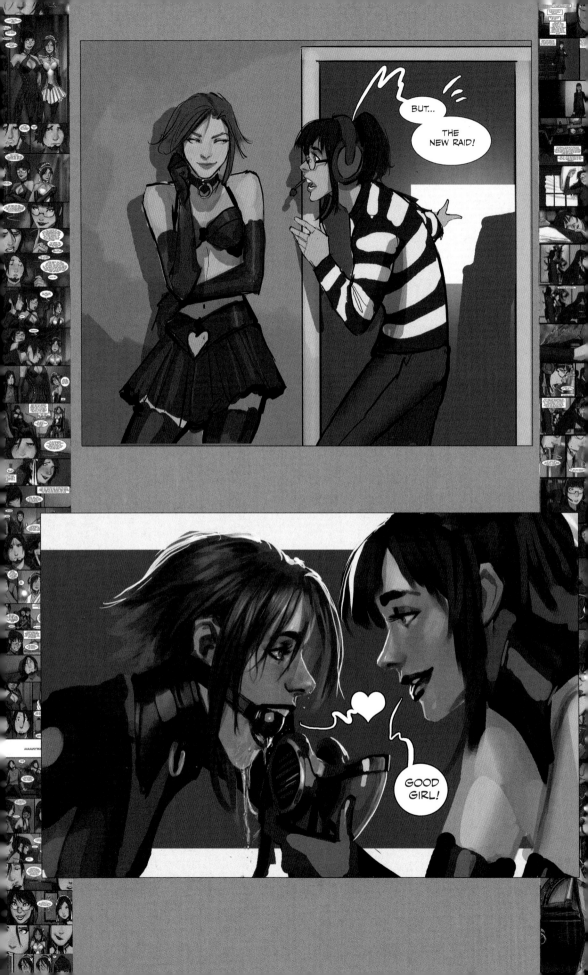

LISTEN...COVID TIMES WERE WEIRD.
SHLICK

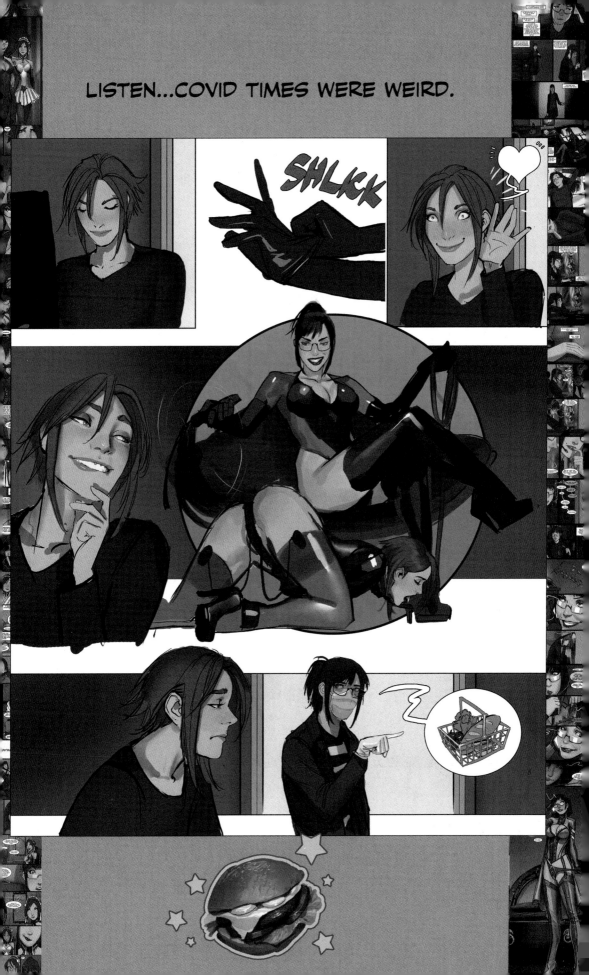

Sunstone
Mercy

UH...YOU FIRST?
DO!
DO NOT!
TRY!

AAAANYWAYS...

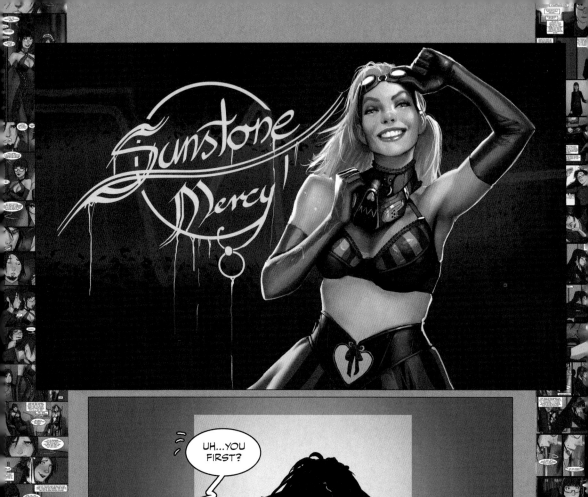

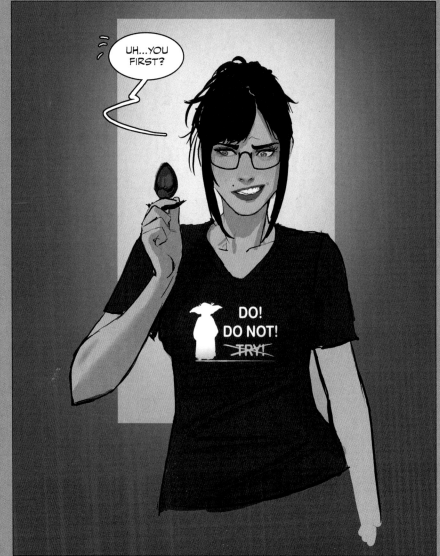

Sunstone
Mercy
TILL DEATH DO US PART
AND BEYOND

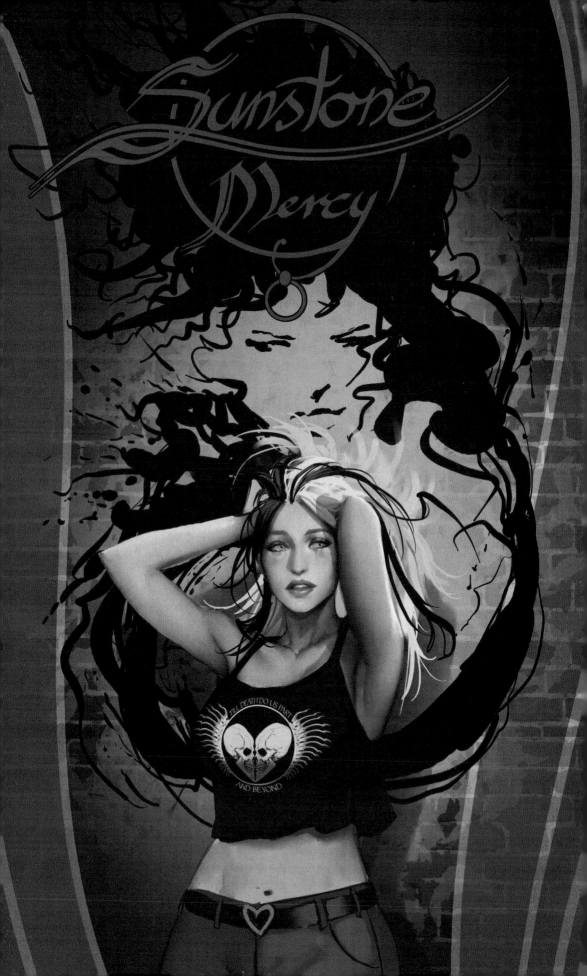

The Top Cow essentials checklist:

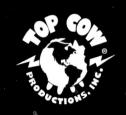

A Man Among Ye, Volume 1
(ISBN: 978-1-5343-1691-1)

Aphrodite IX: Rebirth, Volume 1
(ISBN: 978-1-60706-828-0)

Blood Stain, Volume 1
(ISBN: 978-1-63215-544-3)

Bonehead, Volume 1
(ISBN: 978-1-5343-0664-6)

Cyber Force: Awakening, Volume 1
(ISBN: 978-1-5343-0980-7)

The Clock, Volume 1
(ISBN: 978-1-5343-1611-9)

The Darkness: Origins, Volume 1
(ISBN: 978-1-60706-097-0)

Death Vigil, Volume 1
(ISBN: 978-1-63215-278-7)

Dissonance, Volume 1
(ISBN: 978-1-5343-0742-1)

Eclipse, Volume 1
(ISBN: 978-1-5343-0038-5)

Eden's Fall, Volume 1
(ISBN: 978-1-5343-0065-1)

The Freeze, OGN
(ISBN: 978-1-5343-1211-1)

God Complex, Volume 1
(ISBN: 978-1-5343-0657-8)

Infinite Dark, Volume 1
(ISBN: 978-1-5343-1056-8)

La Voz de M.A.Y.O.:
Tato Rambo, Volume 1
(ISBN: 978-1-5343-1363-7)

Paradox Girl, Volume 1
(ISBN: 978-1-5343-1220-3)

Port of Earth, Volume 1
(ISBN: 978-1-5343-0646-2)

Postal, Volume 1
(ISBN: 978-1-63215-342-5)

Stairway Anthology
(ISBN: 978-1-5343-1702-4)

Sugar, Volume 1
(ISBN: 978-1-5343-1641-7)

Sunstone, Volume 1
(ISBN: 978-1-63215-212-1)

Swing, Volume 1
(ISBN: 978-1-5343-0516-8)

Symmetry, Volume 1
(ISBN: 978-1-63215-699-0)

The Tithe, Volume 1
(ISBN: 978-1-63215-324-1)

Think Tank, Volume 1
(ISBN: 978-1-60706-660-6)

Vindication, OGN
(ISBN: 978-1-5343-1237-1)

Warframe, Volume 1
(ISBN: 978-1-5343-0512-0)

Witchblade 2017, Volume 1
(ISBN: 978-1-5343-0685-1)

For more ISBN and ordering information on our latest collections go to:
www.topcow.com
Ask your retailer about our catalogue of collected editions, digests, and hard covers
or check the listings at: Barnes and Noble, Amazon.com, and other fine retailers.

To find your nearest comic shop go to:
www.comicshoplocator.com